Taken
by Rosemary Hayes

Published by Raven Books
An imprint of Ransom Publishing Ltd.
Unit 7, Brocklands Farm, West Meon, Hampshire GU32 1JN, UK
www.ransom.co.uk

ISBN   978 178591 358 7
First published in 2017

Taken

Rosemary Hayes

RAVEN

One

What if she'd gone home the usual way?

Turned right outside the school gates, not left?

Would everything have stayed the same?

But she hadn't, had she? She'd gone the long way round, across the park, walking slowly, kicking out at the fallen leaves and daydreaming about Mark Ryley, the fittest boy in school.

Stop it, Kelly Wilson, he's way out of your league.

Still, no harm in a bit of fantasising. She could dream, couldn't she? Imagine a moment when she dropped something and he picked it up, his hand brushing hers as he gave it back to her, then their eyes meeting …

She sighed.

Idiot. That is SO not going to happen!

She'd only come this way because she was on her own.

Usually she walked home with Lizzie, but Lizzie was at drama club.

Lizzie would have stopped her.

'Don't go there, Kell. It makes you sad.'

Aren't I allowed to be sad?

Dad. He'd gone four years ago, at exactly this time of year and on a day like this, a still, sunny Autumn day, the air heavy with the scent of ripening berries.

Kelly walked slowly over to the chestnut tree – *their* chestnut tree. She'd been here with Dad ever since she could remember, in every season, sheltering under it, sitting against its huge trunk, playing games around it. There were conkers spread on the ground beneath it, shiny and unmarked, bursting out of their spiky shells. Kelly shrugged her bag off her shoulder and squatted down to pick some up, then sat back on her heels, staring at them lying in her hand, the memory still strong even after all this time.

The memory of that day, when Dad had been sitting right here beside her, gently stroking the gleaming sheen on the conkers before stuffing them into his pockets.

'Too lovely to leave.' Then he'd looked at her and suddenly turned his head away.

At the time she'd thought nothing of it, but afterwards …

Kelly's eyes filled with tears and angrily she wiped her eyes with the back of her hand.

How many times had she played those words over in her head?

She squatted there for a while, then sighed and got slowly to her feet and, as she did so, a tiny movement caught her eye.

It was so slight that she could easily have missed it – just a shifting of shadows in the distance, at the edge of the woods surrounding the park.

Her eyes were still bleary with tears as she whipped her head round, the skin at the back of her neck prickling, sensing she was being watched.

Oh god, it'll be Lycra Ted!

But Lycra Ted didn't usually lurk in the shadows. If he'd seen her he would have jogged over, puffing and wheezing from the effort. He was seriously boring, always looking for an excuse to stop and chat.

Lycra Ted was another reason why she and Lizzie didn't come home this way.

Kelly looked round. There was no one else in the park. Not even kids in the play area. Just her luck! There was some perv over in the woods – otherwise she was on her own. She shivered as she grabbed her bag and made a dash for the gates.

She was almost there, close to the gates and the road – where there were cars and people – when she stopped and looked back again.

Had she imagined it?

You're just jumpy because there's no one else around.

But as she stared, she saw that there *was* someone there. Almost impossible to distinguish from the shadows, until the tall figure (a man, surely?) moved and became briefly separated from his surroundings, before he turned away and was absorbed back into the darkness of the trees.

She saw it as he turned. Something about the set of his shoulders and the way he moved – not with an even stride, but with that stiffness in his right leg.

The stab of familiarity made her gasp.

For a moment she forgot how to breathe and felt her heart banging hard against her ribcage. She made a weak cry and took a few steps in his direction, her fist clenched tight against the conkers in her hand.

Her brain told her it couldn't be him. It wasn't possible. And yet ...

Don't!

Kelly flung the conkers to the ground and raced for the gates. She should never have come home this way. Stupid! Stupid! Stupid!

She stopped when she was out of the park and stood by the railings, taking great gulping breaths.

What had she seen, after all? Some man she thought was her dad.

'You're nuts,' she told herself. 'It wasn't him. You *know* it couldn't have been him. It was just some perv. Which is why, Kelly Wilson, it is not a great idea to walk back from school through the park on your own.'

When she reached her house, her breathing had slowed but her cheeks were still red and her eyes puffy. She tried to slink upstairs to her room, but Gran was there at the kitchen door, a tea-towel slung over her shoulder.

'Good day at school?'

As if she cares!

'Fine,' said Kelly, her foot on the first stair.

Gran frowned and came closer. Kelly started up the stairs. 'Not so fast, young lady. Let me look at you.'

Kelly sighed. 'Nothing to look at, Gran. I'm just the same as when I left this morning.'

'That's enough of your cheek.' Gran frowned. 'Have you been crying?'

'No.'

Gran ignored her. 'Something wrong at school?'

'No,' Kelly shouted. Then she ran upstairs and into her bedroom, slamming the door behind her. She put some music on, turned it up loud, then flung herself down on her bed.

Idiot. Forget it. Whoever you saw, it wasn't him.

But the image stayed with her, and that night she dreamt of him. When it had happened, she'd often dreamt of her dad and woken up sobbing, until Mum heard her and came in to comfort her. But she'd not dreamt of him for ages.

The next morning Mum was in the kitchen working at her laptop and Gran was leaning over her shoulder, making suggestions. Kelly could sense the tension in the air. Mum was trying not to show her irritation; she looked up when Kelly came into the room and closed the laptop.

'Hi love,' she said. 'Sorry I was so late last night. I'd hoped to get in before you went to bed, but the meeting went on and then there was this dinner thing … '

'Yeah. Whatever.' Kelly didn't look at her and instead started making herself a drink.

'Still grumpy,' said Gran, folding her arms. 'She hardly spoke a word at tea last night. It's the hormones.'

Mum got up and came over to Kelly. 'You OK, love?' she said quietly.

Kelly shrugged her off. 'I'm *fine!*'

She immediately felt guilty. Mum was keeping them all together, going out to work, earning the money, putting up with Gran (who told her twenty times a day how to bring up her children) and still trying to be there for the two of them – her and Nathan.

'See,' said Gran. 'She's nearly fifteen and still not learnt any manners.' Then she went off on one of her child-rearing rants and Kelly tuned out.

'Sorry Mum,' she whispered. 'Didn't sleep too well.'

Mum smiled and briefly squeezed her shoulder.

Nathan shuffled into the room, yawning, his hair still tousled. He was clutching his phone and he didn't say anything, but headed for the fridge and took out a carton of juice.

Gran started on him. 'Don't bother to say good morning, Nathan.'

Nathan frowned and briefly focused. 'Uh. Oh, hi.'

Gran let out a loud sigh.

Some toast popped up and Kelly took a slice and sat down at the table. She looked from Mum to Nathan. Nathan had Mum's thick shiny hair – wasted on a boy – and regular features, even if they were covered in spots. And he was fine-boned, like her. Whereas she – Kelly – was tall and gangly with wild curly auburn hair. It was all the wrong way round. Mum said she had lovely eyes, but she was just being kind. What she didn't say was that she was a dead ringer for her dad.

Her dad.

Stop it! Stop thinking about it!

Nathan sat down and gulped his juice, still staring at his phone, constantly scrolling down. He didn't even look up when

Mum put a plate of scrambled eggs in front of him, but just began stabbing at it with a fork with his free hand, his eyes still glued to his phone.

Kelly sighed.

It was hard to believe that she and Nathan were brother and sister. They were from different planets. And, thank god, they were at different schools. Nathan was a geek and he'd got a scholarship to a fancy school the other side of town.

Kelly glanced at the clock on the wall. She scraped back her chair, kissed Mum, then ran out of the kitchen, grabbing her coat and bag from the hall as she went.

'Bye,' she yelled, as she opened the front door. 'See you later.'

Lizzie lived at the other end of the street.

'How's things?' she said, as they set off together.

Kelly pulled a face. 'Gran's ranting about my manners and Nathan's a smelly geek.'

'No change, then.'

Kelly grinned and shook her head. 'How was drama club?'

'Yeah. Good. I got the starring role!'

'Hey that's fantastic. What is it?'

Lizzie rolled her eyes. 'How many times have I told you? We're doing Romeo and Juliet.'

'Oh yeah. So you're, like, Juliet?'

'Duh! *Obviously.*'

'Who's Romeo then?'

For a second, Lizzie hesitated. She looked down.

'Mark Ryley,' she said.

Kelly swallowed, fighting back a wave of jealousy.

'So, what, you'll be snogging him and everything?'

Lizzie punched her on the arm. 'It's a *play*, you idiot. As in pretend – not real.'

'Yeah, 'course it is.'

Kelly sneaked a look at Lizzie. She was dead pretty, small with huge brown eyes framed by long sleek dark hair. Mark was sure to fancy her. How could he not? Suddenly Kelly felt miserable. Her life was crap. Gran was a nightmare, Nathan was on another planet, Mum was hardly ever at home and now Mark would fall in love with her best friend. She sighed.

Who am I kidding? Mark would never fancy me anyway. Not in a million years.

They walked on in silence for a few minutes, Kelly frowning and staring at the ground.

'What's wrong?' asked Lizzie. 'You're not upset about Mark and me being in the play are you?'

Kelly shook her head. 'No, it's not … ' Then suddenly she started to cry.

'Sorry.' She stopped walking and fished a tissue out of her pocket. She blew her nose. 'I don't know … I'm all over the place.'

Lizzie took her arm. 'What is it?'

'Nothing. I'll feel better tomorrow. Gran says it's my hormones.'

Lizzie snorted. 'Typical!'

Kelly didn't answer and began to walk on.

Lizzie caught her up. 'Come on, Kell. What's up?'

Kelly sniffed, then raised her head and met Lizzie's eyes.

'If I tell you, will you promise not to say anything?'

'Hey, that sounds heavy. You're not pregnant, are you?'

Kelly smiled through her tears. 'Yeah, like a virgin birth!'

Lizzie grinned. 'Phew! Thought maybe there was something you weren't telling me.'

'No. Nothing like that. But you really *can't* tell anyone, Lizzie. Promise?'

'OK.'

'It's so stupid.'

'Go on.'

Kelly wiped her eyes with the back of her hand. 'Yesterday, I walked back from school through the park.'

'Idiot! Did some perv flash you?'

'Shut up! No, it was worse.'

Lizzie's eyes were wide. 'Worse! Oh my god!'

'Not that kind of worse.' Kelly hesitated. 'I … I thought I saw my dad.'

Lizzie said nothing for a moment, then, gently, 'You know that's not possible.'

Kelly nodded. 'I know. I thought that too.'

'You told me you used to imagine seeing him, after it first happened.'

'Yeah. But that was a long time ago. I haven't done that for ages. Yesterday was different.'

'How?'

So Kelly told her what she'd seen.

Lizzie frowned. 'Did you say anything to your mum?'

'Are you mad? Can you imagine what that would do to her?'

'You never talk about him at home, do you?'

Kelly shook her head. 'Not really.' She started walking again, her hands in her pockets. 'If he'd died *normally* – you know, been hit by a car or something – then perhaps we could. It's just the way it happened ... '

Lizzie fell into step beside her. 'You don't see that counsellor any more do you?'

'You *know* I don't!'

'Would it be ... '

Kelly turned, her eyes hard. 'What? You think I'm going mental again? I tell you, Lizzie, I didn't imagine it.'

She'd long ago accepted that her dad was dead, but what happened yesterday was different. She'd not been looking for him like she had in the past – and then suddenly he'd been there. Hadn't he?

'OK. I'm sorry,' said Lizzie. 'So, what are you going to do?'

'You believe me?'

Lizzie looked down at the ground. 'If you believe it, then I believe it.' She hesitated. 'Are you going to tell anyone else what you saw?'

Kelly shook her head.

'You're just going to leave it, then?'

'Dunno. 'S'pose so.'

They walked on in silence for a while and then Lizzie cleared her throat. She spoke slowly. 'They found his clothes on that beach, Kelly. And the note.'

'I *know* that. But they never found his body, did they?'

'Oh Kelly!' Lizzie put an arm round her.

'It's just that ... '

'What?'

'Well, he might not be dead. He might still be alive. He *could* be, couldn't he?'

They'd arrived at the school gates so Lizzie didn't answer, and as they went into the yard Kelly whispered. 'Promise you won't say anything?'

''Course not,' said Lizzie, but later, as she watched Kelly hang up her coat, she frowned to herself.

Would she be able to keep that promise? What if Kelly was losing it again?

Two

When Kelly got back from school that afternoon, there was no one in the house except Gran, who was standing in the passage wriggling into her jacket, car keys clutched in one hand, her large black handbag jammed under one arm and two supermarket bags dangling from her other hand.

'I need to get to the supermarket. I was going earlier but then that woman, what's-her-name from next door, came round and … '

Gran sniffed and headed down the hall. At the door she turned. 'I'll be back before Nathan's home. He's at chess club.'

Chess club. Of course he is. The only social life he has, the nerd.

Aloud, Kelly said, 'Sure. See you later.'

She fetched a drink and some biscuits and went upstairs to her room. The door to Gran's bedroom was open and she hesitated outside and peered in. Gran had come to live with them not long after Dad had gone, but even after all this time it still upset her seeing all Gran's stuff in there. It had been Dad's studio. It was where he used to work, and there was still the faintest whiff of turpentine hanging about the place. Gran moaned that it was impossible to get rid of the smell.

Kelly stood there. She could still see it as it used to be, with the big easel in the middle of the room, where the light from the window was best, and with all the tubes of paints and brushes on a big table and finished canvasses propped up along the walls. She had loved watching him work and he'd never minded, just as long as she didn't talk.

She hardly remembered, now, what had happened after he disappeared. It was all such a blur, with people everywhere – police, relations, friends. And she'd sort of shut down. For ages, the studio had remained untouched, a shrine. They thought he'd turn up, come back to them. No one wanted to move anything, so it was just as he had left it, waiting for him to walk into the room and pick up a paintbrush.

Until they found his clothes – and the note.

Kelly took a deep breath. She *wouldn't* think about it. She *wouldn't* go back there again. She frowned and walked into the room. It had Gran's stamp on it now, her bed neatly made, her clothes in the wardrobe and her hair brush and make-up and lotions and potions all lined up on the dressing table.

Dad's books and CDs – books on painters he'd admired, music he liked to play while he worked – these had all been put away in the attic and now the shelves were full of Gran's things, her ornaments and books. Weirdly, Gran was into murder mysteries and there were loads of them, but she also kept her diaries there. She wrote in her diary every day without fail.

'If I don't go to bed now I'll be too tired to write up my diary,' she'd say, heaving herself off the couch in the lounge and heading for the stairs.

Once, Kelly had sneaked into the room after she and Gran had had a mega row and looked in Gran's diary to see if she'd written anything nasty. But it was dead boring. She'd just put, 'Kelly very bad tempered today', then went on to describe a conversation with some friend of hers who had had an operation.

Kelly looked at her watch. Gran wouldn't be back any time soon – nor would Nathan. She scanned the row of diaries – one book for each year, going back ages – and took out the one written four years ago. She turned the pages until she came to the day her dad had vanished. The entry was very short.

October 10th
   Steve's disappeared. Jen phoned in a terrible state. Everyone worried sick.

Kelly turned the page.

October 11th
   Didn't sleep a wink last night. Went round to Jen's first thing. Family liaison woman there with the children. Poor kids. Kelly hysterical. Police coming and going all day. Still no word from Steve. Hope to god that other business hasn't started up again.

Kelly frowned, the diary suddenly heavy in her hands. What other business? What did she mean?

She forced herself to read on, day after day of that dreadful time. It was all there, starkly described. One or two of the entries just read, *Still no news* and then, a month after he'd disappeared, another entry, the writing unsteady.

> *They've found his clothes on a beach. He'd left a note apparently. If he could see what he's done to his family.*

Kelly angrily snapped the diary shut and replaced it on the shelf. She couldn't bear to read any more. But the phrase 'that other business' wouldn't go away.

She picked up another diary from another year, scanning it for references to Dad, but she couldn't find anything to indicate he'd been in any trouble, or he and Mum had fallen out or anything. And anyway, the police had been over and over his life – so had the Press – and they couldn't find any reason why he'd done it.

She sat down in Gran's armchair. It was a long time since she'd allowed herself to think back to the weeks after he'd disappeared. It was so confused in her head; all of them in shock, the house full of random people, being off school and then, when she'd gone back, kids avoiding her, not knowing what to say. Except Lizzie. Lizzie had always been there for her.

After a while she got up, but instead of going into her room she pulled down the roof ladder and climbed up into the attic.

The attic wasn't big and you could only stand up in the

middle, the roof pitching sharply on either side. She looked round and saw a load of boxes and cases piled on top of one another and, against the end wall, some neatly stacked canvasses. She went closer and squatted down, turning them over, one by one, then, with a jolt, she saw the painting he'd done not long before he'd disappeared. She could picture it on his easel and remembered him standing back, looking at it with that quizzical expression on his face, a paintbrush clamped between his teeth.

Although he'd had it framed, he'd left it there sitting on the easel, and for weeks after he'd gone his presence was still with them in that painting and in the overpowering smell of turpentine.

Carefully, she removed the painting from the others and looked at it. It was quite big and it wasn't in his usual style, and as she stared at it, she remembered something he'd said when she'd asked him who it was for.

Just for me, this one.

Kelly sat there for ages, holding the painting, the memories of him flooding back.

Oh Dad!

Then she noticed the time. Gran would be back soon and she didn't want to face an inquisition about why she was in the attic. She picked up the painting and, holding it carefully under one arm, climbed down the ladder and onto the upstairs landing. She swung the ladder back into place and took the painting into her room.

She could see it better there. She stared at it for a long time, frowning. It was much more impressionistic than his usual work, but she recognised where it was. The autumn colours were vibrant – yellows and reds – and the painting looked as fresh today as when it had been propped on his easel.

It was the park. He'd never sat out in the park painting, she was sure of it. This was from memory.

It was a while before she made out the figures. A child and a man sitting beneath a tree. And another, much vaguer figure, hidden in the shadows at the edge of the wood, hardly discernable, unless you were looking for it.

Just like this afternoon. She shivered.

You knew, Dad. Even then, you knew you were going to leave us.

The front door slammed and Kelly jumped.

'I'm back, Kelly. Come and give me a hand with the shopping.'

She slipped the painting under her bed and ran downstairs.

'That girl on the checkout was so rude,' said Gran. 'Didn't even answer me when I asked about something. Just rang for the supervisor. No manners.'

'If you'd use the scanner, you wouldn't have to go through the checkout, Gran. It's a lot quicker that way.'

'Huh! Don't trust those things.'

Kelly sighed and started unpacking and putting away the shopping.

'That other business.' What did it mean?

She glanced over at Gran, who was muttering about the price of cheese.

Why did she put that in her diary? What does she know?

Kelly's phone pinged and she dragged it out of her pocket. A text from Lizzie.

Suddenly, all thoughts of her dad vanished.

Gran frowned. 'Who's that from?'

'Only Lizzie.'

As if it's any of your business.

'Why are you blushing, then?'

It was true. As soon as she'd read it, the colour had flamed her face.

'I am *not* blushing.'

Nosy old bat!

Gran raised an eyebrow and said nothing, but she didn't need to. Kelly knew what she was thinking. *Hormones!*

She couldn't believe it! Mark was having a Halloween party at the end of the month and he'd asked Lizzie to come – and bring a friend.

She replied as soon as Gran's back was turned, the text full of symbols and asterisks.

The reply came back instantly.

That's a yes then?!

Kelly smiled to herself.

'Stop dreaming, girl!' snapped Gran. 'Look what you've done.'

'Whoops! Sorry!' Kelly started to giggle as she fished the cereal out of the fridge and put it in the cupboard.

Gran narrowed her eyes. 'It's a boy, isn't it?'

'What? What are you on about?'

'The text. It was a boy.'

'No it was *not!*'

She's a witch. How does she know?

A witch. She could go to the party as a witch – but maybe that was too obvious? Kelly stood clutching a tub of ice cream.

'Wake up Kelly!'

Kelly came back to earth and put the ice cream in the freezer.

Mum came home early and for once they all ate together. Most of the time, Kelly was thinking about Mark's party, and she was texting Lizzie as she ate, her phone on her lap, out of Gran's sight.

Mum cleared her throat. 'I was thinking about Christmas,' she said.

Kelly and Gran both looked up. The last few Christmasses had been hard, and Kelly was already dreading the next one. Mum had tried – and so had Gran, to be fair – but Dad's absence was palpable. All the jobs he'd done, the silly things he'd written on presents, the pictures he'd drawn for them – and when he'd lit the brandy round the Christmas pudding, it had always been a disaster; either the flames were so high he had to smother them, or there was just one tiny spluttering flame that went out immediately.

Mum went on. 'John and Emma have invited us.'

What!

She'd got their full attention. Even Nathan looked up. 'But you don't even *like* them,' he said.

John was Dad's brother. He was a businessman with a glamorous wife and two children who were much older than Kelly and Nathan – and he lived in this fancy house miles away.

Mum swallowed. 'That's not true, Nat. It's just that … well, we don't have much in common. But it's kind of them to ask us.' And, as Gran started to moan, she went on, 'Just hear me out will you, Mum. We won't be staying with them.'

'Too right we won't,' muttered Nathan.

'There's this cottage in the village. The owners will be away over Christmas and they want someone to house-sit and look after the animals.'

'Animals?' Kelly perked up. 'What animals?'

'A dog and a cat I think.'

Gran started to stack the dishes. 'I think it's a lot of upheaval,' she said firmly. 'Much easier to stay here.'

'Well … ' said Mum slowly, 'It might be good to have a change of scene.'

There was a heavy silence and the unspoken thoughts were loud in the room. Away from this house, where Dad had always spent Christmas. A break with the memories.

'It would be good to have animals to look after,' said Kelly at last.

Mum smiled. 'I thought you'd like that.' She hesitated. 'So, shall I say *yes*?'

'Would we have to see Ned and Matilda?' Nathan had always felt intimidated by his confident cousins.

'I expect they'll be busy with their friends. We could do our own thing. Though,' Mum hesitated, 'we'd spend Christmas Day with them, of course.'

Gran hauled a dessert out of the fridge and dumped it on the table. 'Humph!'

'Less work for you, Gran,' said Kelly, sweetly.

She'd got her there. Although Gran moaned about doing the full Christmas dinner, Kelly knew she secretly enjoyed it, but she'd never admit it.

Gran said nothing.

'Good,' said Mum. 'I'll say yes then,' and before anyone could speak, she had pinged back an email. Then she closed her phone and leant back in her chair.

After they'd eaten, Gran went out to visit a neighbour and Mum went into her office to do some work. Kelly and Nathan sat in the lounge, both glued to their phones. For a while neither of them spoke, then Kelly looked up.

'Nat?'

'Umm.'

'How d'you feel about Christmas?'

Nathan shrugged. 'I don't much want to see Ned and Matlida, but I s'pose if it's only for the one day.'

'Aw c'mon, they're not that bad.'

'Ned only talks about girls.'

At least he talks!

Kelly took a deep breath. 'D'you think it will help?'

'What d'you mean?'

He knows what I mean.

'Having Christmas in a different place.'

She could see the flush rising on Nathan's face, but she went on.

'Maybe it won't be so bad, Nat.' She hesitated, then said softly, 'Not so many memories of Dad.'

Nathan didn't answer. He lowered his head and stabbed at his phone.

I shouldn't have tried. He won't talk about him.

She'd not seen John and Emma for ages – not since Dad went – and she had forgotten exactly where they lived. She googled the name of the village and saw it was over a hundred miles away and not far from the coast. Vaguely she remembered going for walks along a sea wall when they'd last been there. Maybe she could take the dog for walks by the sea. She looked at the names of coastal villages nearby, but none were familiar. Then she made the map smaller so she could see the nearest town. What else was there to do around there? And as she was peering at the map, a name jumped out at her.

Dunwich!

She stared at it. A tiny dot on the map. Right on the coast.

She closed her eyes, fighting back the feeling of revulsion.

It was a name she could never forget. She turned her phone off and saw that her hands were shaking.

Why did I never realise it was near where they live? It can't be more than ten miles from their house.

She shivered. Dunwich. Where they'd found his clothes – and the note.

How could Mum even *think* of going there – so close to where it all happened?

Three

Kelly went into town at the weekend and she and Lizzie hung out with some other girls from school, trying on clothes and sitting in a café, making their drinks last for ever as they giggled and chatted.

'You're so lucky, Lizzie,' said one of the girls. 'Getting to snog Mark Ryley.'

Lizzie blushed. 'How many times? It's just a play.'

'Still. The hottest guy in school. How good is that?'

Lizzie didn't mention Mark's party to the others.

'Poor guy!' said another. 'D'you think he knows we all talk about him?'

Kelly didn't say anything. She wished they wouldn't go on about him. It was as if he was public property.

'He's probably really shy,' said Lizzie.

'Huh! Can't be. Not looking like that.'

'I'll tell you when I get to know him better,' said Lizzie.

'*Ooo, "get to know him better",*' they chorused.

'Shut up. You know what I mean.'

As the others chatted and giggled, Kelly's thoughts drifted away. She couldn't get those words of Gran's out of her head. *That other business.*

After a while the other girls left, and Kelly and Lizzie were alone.

'I'd better get back,' said Lizzie, standing up and slipping her arms into her coat. 'You coming?'

Kelly shook her head. 'I want to check something out at the library.'

'The library! Can't you find it online?'

'It's for this project,' said Kelly vaguely.

'Project? What project?'

She knows too much about me.

Kelly sighed. 'OK, it's not about a project. It's just an idea I had. Something about my dad.'

Lizzie sat down again. She reached over the table and took Kelly's hand.

'Leave it, Kell. You'll only upset yourself.'

She remembers when I was really bad – when I spent all that time with the counsellor.

'No, I won't. It's just something's been bugging me. Something I read in Gran's diary.'

'You read her diary?'

Kelly grinned. 'Yeah. I know. It was mostly dead boring, but there was this thing she said, when Dad disappeared.'

Then she told Lizzie.

Lizzie frowned. 'But what can you find out from the library?'

Kelly bit her lip. 'I dunno. I just thought I could look up the old local papers, see if he's mentioned.'

'But you could find out online. Our whole lives are out there, for goodness sake.'

'I tried that last night, but it's just the same old stuff – about his paintings and his "suicide".' Kelly held up her fingers to make quotes round the word.

'Shall I come with you?'

'No. It's probably nothing anyway. I just want to … you know.'

'OK, babe. But don't go upsetting yourself.'

Lizzie stood up again. When she reached the door, she turned back and waved. Kelly raised her hand, then watched her as she walked away down the street.

Kelly left a few moments later and headed off towards the central library.

She's right. I shouldn't drag all this up again. I'll just check out the newspapers.

At the library, Kelly asked about back copies of the local paper, pretending she wanted to see them for a school project.

'I looked for them online last night and I couldn't find them,' she said to the librarian.

The woman smiled. 'We don't put all the archive stuff out there,' she said. 'But you can access them with our password.'

Kelly concentrated on the month leading up to her dad's disappearance, trawling through reports of school plays, fêtes, swimming galas, arguments about local planning applications, and minor crimes. She started yawning.

SO boring!

She found nothing. But then she had no idea what she was looking for.

That other business.

She stretched her arms above her head and tried to stop her eyes from closing.

One more time. I'll just flip through them one more time.

The police reports were all on the back page. She decided to go through these more carefully and not bother about anything else.

She'd seen them all before, but had just skimmed the headlines. This time she looked through the articles – and even then, she nearly missed it.

PUB BRAWL

On Tuesday, the police were called to an incident outside the Queen's Head pub in Canal Street, where local artist, Stephen Wilson, sustained facial injuries having been attacked by a fellow drinker. The attacker was not present when the police arrived and Mr Wilson did not wish to press charges.

Kelly was suddenly wide awake. A fight! Her gentle, peace-loving dad had been in a fight! She couldn't picture it. It was SO not like her dad, getting into a fight. And who was the other guy? Why had he attacked Dad?

And why didn't she remember it? *Facial injuries.* Surely she would have remembered if Dad had been beaten up, his face all bruised? She stared at the date again. It was in the summer, a couple of months before Dad disappeared. She would have been – what – ten. She tried to think back. It was in August, so holiday time. But Dad always came on holiday with them.

Then she remembered. That year he'd not gone with them. Mum had been furious with him, but he'd said he was behind with work or something. Mum had tried to explain it to her and Nat, and they'd been really disappointed.

So, did Mum not know about the incident? Surely Dad would have told her? And wouldn't it have come up when he'd disappeared? Anyway, it sounded as though Gran knew about it (*that business*) and she was such an old sticky-beak, she would have told Mum.

Or would she?

And why would anyone get into a *fight* with Dad?

Kelly continued to sit there for a while, staring at the screen, thinking. Then she checked her watch. She'd be late home and Mum would start to worry. She texted her.

Sorry, got held up. Back soon.

She was still deep in thought as she left the library.

'Hello, Kelly.'

She stopped on the steps outside the building and turned round.

At first she didn't recognise the woman who was smiling at her, then it clicked. She used to work with Mum ages ago and she'd been round to the house a couple of times.

Kelly answered all the boring questions – how was school, what did she want to do after she left – even though, all the time, the words were repeating themselves in her mind. *Dad in a fight!*

Just as she was thinking she'd never get away, the clock on the library building struck one and she looked up at it. The woman smiled.

'I must let you go, Kelly,' she said. 'Give your mum my love. I never see her these days, since she went freelance.'

Freelance? She never told me she'd gone freelance.

Kelly ran down the steps onto the pavement and, as she turned to wave, she noticed a man leaning against the entrance to the library, his face obscured by a newspaper.

If she'd still been looking when he lowered the newspaper she would have seen him walk back through the doors. And she might even have recognised him as the man who had been sitting behind her while she trawled through the back copies of the local paper.

She rushed down the steps, her mind still reeling at the thought of her dad involved in any sort of violence, and she wasn't looking as she started to cross the road. A car had to swerve to avoid her and the driver leant on his horn as she jumped back onto the pavement.

Kelly got the bus back home and walked slowly up the road to her house. Gran was out and Mum was in the kitchen chopping vegetables for their tea. She looked up and smiled when Kelly came into the room.

'I saw that woman who used to work with you,' said Kelly, as she took off her coat and hung it in the hall.

Mum stopped chopping for a moment, then continued,

the knife hitting the chopping board with monotonous precision.

'Who was that?'

'Can't remember her name. Youngish, fair with specs.'

'Oh, Anne.' A slight hesitation. 'Did she speak to you?'

Kelly nodded. 'She said you'd gone freelance.'

Mum continued chopping. Kelly went on.

'She said we must like seeing more of you.'

Mum sighed. She put down the knife and wiped her hands on a piece of kitchen towel, then she smoothed back her hair.

'Look love, I'm sorry. P'raps I should have told you.'

'Told me what?'

'About going freelance. I'd hoped it would mean having more time to spend with you and Nat, but it's just not happened.'

Kelly frowned. 'But if you're freelance, don't you work from home? Isn't that what it means?'

Mum smiled and shook her head. 'I go all over the place. Wherever I'm needed,' she said. 'And I've got more work than ever.'

Kelly sat down at the kitchen table. 'So that's good, is it?'

Mum put her hands on Kelly's shoulders. 'Yes. As long as it lasts. But the downside is, I don't get paid when I'm not working.'

Then Mum talked about other things, subtly putting an end to any more questions about her work. Not long afterwards, Gran came back and started telling them about her unsuccessful shopping expedition and the wicked price of shoes.

Kelly laid the table, letting the conversation drift over her head.

There was no reason why Mum should have told her about going freelance, was there? But, all the same …

After tea, Gran announced that she was going to the cinema.

'Why don't you go with Gran?' said Mum, turning to Kelly. 'Keep her company.'

Gran opened her mouth to say something, but closed it again as Mum scowled at her.

Kelly raised her eyebrows. She'd had more than enough of Gran's company.

'No, I've got stuff to do,' she said.

'Homework?' asked Gran, her voice heavy with sarcasm.

'Sort of,' said Kelly. 'I'm researching a project.'

That's shut her up.

But as Gran got ready to go out, she felt a pang of self pity.

Saturday night and it's my gran who's going out, not me. How sad is that?

She left Nathan and Mum watching something on TV and made her way slowly up the stairs. When she heard the front door bang shut, she crept down the passage and into Gran's room. Again, she picked up the diary from four years ago, but this time she looked further back, to August, to when she, Mum and Nat had been on holiday and Dad had stayed at home. To the date when Dad had got into the fight at the Queen's Head.

She turned the pages carefully. At first, she thought she'd turned over several at once.

But she hadn't. The pages for that day, and for three days after, were missing. Deliberately removed with a sharp knife.

Kelly stood very still, the diary open at the non-existent pages, her heart thudding.

She knows something.

Perhaps she should just ask Gran why she'd removed those pages. But immediately she dismissed the idea. Gran would never forgive her for snooping.

After several minutes, she put the diary back in its place on the shelf, tiptoed out of the room, turning off the light and closing the door softly behind her.

Back in her own room, she knelt down and took Dad's picture out and propped it up against the wall. She stood looking at it for several minutes, her hands on her hips.

What was going on, Dad? Who was the man at the pub?

Then she took a deep breath and angrily shoved it back under the bed.

Stop it Kelly. You're going to drive yourself mad. You're going to go back into that bad place again.

The counsellor, the medication, the terrible nightmares.

Leave it. Dad's dead. Whatever you find out, he's never coming back. Nothing's going to change. Get used to it.

And yet …

STOP IT.

Think about Mark's party and what to wear for it.

Four

In the days that followed, Kelly tried her best not to think about her dad. After all, she'd done it before, shutting all thoughts of him away, closing down that part of her memory. She avoided going anywhere near the park and concentrated on doing all the normal school things. Once, Lizzie said to her 'You OK, Kell? You're not still thinking about … *you know?*'

Kelly had shaken her head. 'No. It was … I just had a wobble. I'm fine now.'

'You sure?'

'Sure.'

'Good. Because I need you to concentrate. I have had *the* most brilliant idea.'

'What about?'

'Our costumes for Mark's party.'

'OK.'

'You heard of the Addams Family?'

Kelly frowned. 'Sort of. Weren't there some films?'

Lizzie nodded. 'Gothic horror comedy in the 90s. You could go as Morticia, the mother, and I could go as the daughter, Wednesday.'

'But, will anyone know who we are?'

''Course they will. They're a sort of cult; I've got DVDs of some of the films. Come over to mine and we'll look at them.'

Kelly took some convincing, but she began to warm to the idea.

'You're a shoe-in for Wednesday,' she said, after they'd watched one of the films. 'You've already got the long dark hair and if you parted it in the middle and wore one of those hideous dresses with a collar … '

'And made my face white and my eyebrows huge.'

Kelly giggled. 'Yeah. That too.'

'And you'll be great as Morticia,' said Lizzie. 'You're tall and thin and you can wear a long black dress … '

'And a whitened face and black lippy.'

'And you'll have to hold a lily.'

'And get a wig.'

'Yeah,' laughed Lizzie, 'Curly red hair's *so* not Morticia!'

Kelly hugged Lizzie. 'Hey, it'll be great. Bet we'll be the *only* Addams family. There's sure to be a mass of witches and werewolves and skeletons … '

' … and monsters and ghosts.'

'Wonder what Mark will go as?' said Lizzie. 'I asked him but he said he'd not thought about it.'

'Boys, eh?' said Kelly. 'Too cool to dress up.'

'No. He'll do something at the last minute and it'll be brilliant. You'll see.'

Kelly told her mum about their idea.

'Hey, that's great. I remember the Addams family films. They were hilarious. And I tell you something else.'

'What?'

'You could get your gran to help.'

'Gran!'

Mum nodded. 'She did a lot of acting when she was young – she was really good. She'd have some ideas about what to wear and make-up and that.'

'Gran was an actress?' said Kelly. Somehow she couldn't imagine Gran on stage, strutting her stuff. But then she'd never really thought of her as being young, even. She'd always been – well – just Gran. Overbearing and bossy.

Before Kelly could stop her, Mum was yelling up the stairs, asking Gran to come down.

'We need your help,' she shouted.

Gran came downstairs, grumbling, but when she heard about the Halloween party she smiled and her face relaxed.

'Oh yes, Lizzie will be great as Wednesday, and we'll make you the best Morticia, ever. I'll get all my acting stuff out from the attic.'

Lizzie came over at the weekend. Kelly answered the door.

'Sorry. I couldn't stop her,' she whispered, jerking her thumb back towards the living room. 'Gran's taken over.'

'What?'

'Yeah. But you should see some of the stuff she's hauled out of the attic. It's amazing.'

In the living room, Gran was kneeling beside a huge suitcase, carefully taking things out of tissue paper and draping them over the chairs. She turned round when they came it.

'Look,' she said. 'I've found the perfect dress for Morticia.' She pointed to a long old-fashioned black dress with a high neck and decorated with black lace.'

'That's, like, amazing!' said Lizzie, clapping her hands. 'Put it on Kelly. Let's have a look at you.'

When Kelly was dressed up, Gran started on her make-up, delving into the suitcase for tubes of grease paint. She twisted Kelly's hair back into a knot and began applying a load of white stuff to her face, then made her eyes look huge with black eye shadow.

'I'm sure there's a wig somewhere in here,' she said, when she'd finished on Kelly's face. She rummaged in the case and brought out a long black wig, which she carefully placed on Kelly's head, ramming it down securely. Then she stood back to admire her handiwork.

'Wow!' said Lizzie.

Gran smiled. 'Go and look at yourself in the mirror in the hall.'

Kelly couldn't believe the transformation. 'Gran, it's brilliant. Thank you SO much!'

She threw her arms round Gran, who was still smiling.

'Careful!' she said, as she drew away. 'You'll cover me with your make-up.'

'All you need is a lily and great long nails painted black.'

'Now for you, Lizzie,' said Gran. It wasn't long before she had found a short black dress with a white Peter Pan collar, had parted Lizzie's long dark hair in the middle and put it into sticking-out plaits and, when the make-up was applied, she was a dead ringer for Wednesday.

They had just finished when the front door opened and Mum came into the living room. She stopped when she saw the girls, her hand flying to her mouth.

'That is just *fantastic!*' she said. She turned to Kelly. 'What did I tell you? I knew Gran would help.'

'Help!' said Lizzie. 'She's done it all. She's been brilliant.'

Gran sat down. 'I really enjoyed that,' she said. She pointed at the suitcase. 'I haven't opened it for years. It took me right back.'

'Did you do much acting?' asked Lizzie.

Gran stretched her arms over her head. She nodded. 'Umm. There was a time … '

But then her smile faded. 'Why don't I make us all some tea,' she said, heaving herself out of the chair and padding down the passage to the kitchen.

Kelly turned to her mum. 'Did she really do a lot of acting?'

Mum nodded. 'Umm. She was professional for a while, but then … ' She didn't finish the sentence.

'Then?'

Mum shrugged. 'Life happened. And it was too hard – you know – with a family.'

Later, when they'd taken off the Halloween gear and were up in Kelly's room, Lizzie said, 'You know, I can see your gran as an actress.'

'Umm,' said Kelly, raising her eyes to the ceiling. 'A neurotic temperamental nightmare.'

'That's a bit harsh!'

'You don't have to live with her.' Carefully, Kelly removed the make-up from her face with a tissue. 'But she was great with the costumes, I'll give her that.'

The next week dragged. Kelly was nervous about Mark's party, but at least Lizzie would be there and at least they had something to wear.

Then suddenly it was Saturday night.

Mum had insisted that she drive them to Mark's house and collect them at the end of the party.

'*Mum!*'

'Don't argue,' said Mum firmly. 'You can't go on the bus all dressed up.'

'We can take a cab.'

'No need,' she said.

Kelly had to give in on that one, but she really didn't want her mum hanging around Mark's house embarrassing her.

'OK, then. But just drop us off and pick us up – from outside the house.'

Mum gave her a hard stare and Kelly smiled. 'Sorry. I mean, thanks Mum.'

'That's better. Now what's the address?'

Kelly told her and Mum looked up, surprised. 'You never told me it was the Ryleys giving the party.'

Oh god, she knows his parents. Please don't let her come into the house.

'Didn't know you knew them.'

Mum nodded slowly. 'Not well. I was … I was at college with Ben Ryley. When we first came to live here we saw a bit of them. So, what's his daughter called?'

'His daughter?'

'Isn't his daughter giving the party?'

Kelly shook her head. 'His son.'

'Oh.'

There's was a moment's silence. 'His son. He'd be a couple of years older than you and Lizzie, then?'

Kelly nodded, trying not to blush.

'So, you'll be younger than the others?'

'What's with all these questions, Mum? He's in drama club with Lizzie, that's why we've been invited.'

'I see.' A hesitation, then, 'Will his parents be at the party?'

'I don't know, do I?'

Another silence, then Mum took Kelly's hand. 'Well, be careful, love.'

Kelly shook her off. 'Of course I'll be careful! It's only a Halloween party, Mum, not some sort of orgy.'

'I'll be there to pick you up at eleven,' said Mum.

Kelly was sullen as they drove to Lizzie's house, resenting her mum's probing, suddenly dreading the party, any excited anticipation soured by Mum's comments. But when she saw Lizzie coming out of her house, the light from the hall picking up her whitened features, she had to laugh.

Mum laughed, too, and it broke the tension. 'Wednesday Addams as I live and breathe,' said Mum.

Lizzie got in the car and they drove off.

Mark lived over the other side of town, where the houses were bigger and more spaced out, with large gardens. There was no doubt where the party was. There were lanterns and fluorescent skeletons dangling in the trees in the front garden and flashing lights coming from inside the house.

'Wow!' said Lizzie.

'They've certainly made an effort,' said Mum. She hesitated. 'Shall I wait 'til you're inside?'

'No!' said Kelly. Then, more quietly. 'No, honestly Mum. We'll be fine. See you later.'

She and Lizzie clambered out of the car and walked slowly up the garden path to the front door.

'I won't know anyone,' whispered Kelly.

Lizzie squeezed her hand. 'I'll only know the drama group lot,' said Lizzie. 'Stick with me. You'll be fine.'

But, as they walked in through the open door, Kelly felt out of place. Immediately she could see that most of the other kids there were older than her and Lizzie, and suddenly her outfit seemed stupid and unsophisticated. For a few moments they stood awkwardly in the hall, unsure what to do or where to go. Then Mark came up. He was dressed in a vampire costume – sleeked back hair, a red silk shirt, a cloak and tight black trousers.

He looks more gorgeous up close. Even dressed as a vampire!

Mark frowned, then laughed.

'Lizzie. I didn't recognise you. You look … '

'Wonderful,' said a voice behind them. An older man, who Kelly assumed was Mark's dad, had come out of another room.

'Fantastic costumes,' he said. ' No one else has come as the Addams family.'

'The Addams ... ?' said Mark.

'Great films,' said his dad. 'Gothic funnies from the nineties.'

'Ah. OK. Anyway, come in,' said Mark. He turned to Kelly.'

'You're Kelly, aren't you?'

Kelly nodded, too embarrassed to speak. She felt such an idiot now, with her white face and blackened eyes, not knowing what to do with the lily she was clutching.

'She's Morticia,' said his dad.

'Right.'

Clearly Mark didn't know about the Addams family films. As they walked into the main room and were surrounded by a whole lot of squealing, strutting, laughing older kids (vampires, devils, ghosts and skeletons, all looking so sure of themselves in their masks and costumes), Kelly was suddenly glad that Mark's dad was there. He took them over to a table and handed them a drink each.

'Is it ... ' began Kelly. She wanted to say non-alcoholic, but that sounded so sad.

Mark's dad grinned. 'It's just a punch,' he said. 'Called vampire's blood – but there's no booze in it – or blood for that matter.'

'Thanks,' said Kelly.

Before long, some of Lizzie's friends from drama club turned up and Lizzie started chatting to them. She tried to involve Kelly, but they were all talking about rehearsals and stuff, and after a while Kelly wandered off. She put down her lily, helped herself to another drink and opened doors until she found an empty room; it was obviously the utility room with a washing machine and dryer and a rack with boots in it. She stood against the wall for a bit, then slid down until she was sitting on the floor. She stared around her.

This is SO sad. What am I doing here, staring at a laundry basket, dressed up like an idiot?

She looked at her watch.

Oh god, there's hours to go.

She'd been sitting there for some time when the door opened and a tall boy dressed as a skeleton came in. Kelly recognised him; he was at her school, in Mark's year.

'Oh! Er ... hi,' he muttered. Then, 'You OK?'

Kelly looked up. 'Yeah. I just ... '

What could she say? That she didn't know a soul and felt like an idiot.

'Mind if I sit down?'

She shook her head. 'Sure.'

There wasn't much room and there was some awkward shuffling as the skeleton lowered himself to the floor beside Kelly. She looked at his legs, stuck out in front of him. They seemed to go on for ever.

'Er, I'm Jack.'

'Kelly.'

Jack pointed at her costume. 'Great costume. What ... what's it ... '

' ... s'posed to be?' finished Kelly. She sighed. 'Morticia Addams.'

'Yeah?'

'Addams family. Film from the nineties.'

'Ah. Sorry, I didn't … '

'No. Nobody does.'

Another silence.

'Are you in the drama club.'

Kelly shook her head.

'Me neither,' said Jack. 'I'm just a friend of Mark's.'

Kelly felt herself blushing, but it didn't show under her white make-up.

'Yeah. We go biking together.'

'Biking?' Immediately, Kelly had a vision of tight lycra shorts. She blushed again.

'Racing,' said Jack. 'We're in the same club.'

Kelly tried to think of something to say about racing bikes – and failed.

Jack cleared his throat. 'Are you into … sports … or anything.'

She felt sorry for him. At least he was trying.

'I like swimming.'

'What. Are you in a club or something?'

She shook her head. 'No. I just like it.'

Suddenly she had a clear memory of being on holiday at the coast, she and Dad jumping the waves. She'd been shrieking with laughter, hiccupping. Where had the others been – Mum and Nat? They must have been there too, but she only saw Dad.

Stop it! Why do I keep thinking of him?

She swallowed, aware that Jack had spoken. 'Sorry?'

Just then, the door opened again and Lizzie came in.

'So *that's* where you've been hiding, Kell. I've been looking for you. Come and get some food.'

Jack and Kelly scrambled to their feet and when Kelly stood up she realised how tall Jack was. Not many 16-year-old boys were taller than her.

'I'd better ... ' he began.

Kelly felt sorry for him. 'Come and get something to eat,' she said.

Lizzie gave her a quick look. 'Sure.'

The three of them made their way into the kitchen, where everyone was crowded round a table helping themselves to food. Kelly thought the Halloween theme might be carried on into the food, with gross-looking black jelly or something, but to her relief there were just quiches and salads and sausages and baked potatoes. When they'd loaded their plates they made for the main room, but it was heaving. Kelly caught sight of Mark, his arm draped casually round the shoulders of a very pretty witch.

Why do I even care? He doesn't have a clue who I am anyway.

'There's no room in there,' she said quickly. 'Let's go out in the garden.'

Although it was late October, it wasn't that cold and the lanterns in the trees lit up the fluorescent skeletons which swung from the branches. Along the front wall there were about a dozen hollowed-out pumpkins, each with a ghastly expression illuminated by light inside them.

'They're gross,' said Lizzie, laughing.

'Yeah, but sort of cool, too,' said Kelly.

I would have thought they were babyish if they were anywhere else. But at Mark's place they look right somehow.

They sat along the wall between the pumpkins, and for a while they were the only ones in the garden, but then others began to spill out from the house and suddenly there was a whole crowd outside. Someone turned up the music and opened the windows and a song with a heavy bass beat reverberated all round, diffused slightly by the night air.

It wasn't long before people started dancing and Lizzie, Kelly and Jack joined in, not touching each other but just moving with the music.

Kelly relaxed. It was OK. She didn't feel so alone now, and even when Lizzie greeted someone from the drama club and started dancing with him, she didn't feel deserted. She was glad of Jack's presence and he didn't bother her. He had stopped dancing and was sitting on the wall again, his long legs spread out in front of him, moving to the music and tapping out the rhythm on his knee.

'It's good, isn't it?' he said after a while, and she nodded. 'Yeah. It's nice.'

It seemed no time before cars started to draw up outside the house, doors were slamming and people were shouting goodbye, not wanting their parents to hang about.

Lizzie was beside her now. 'I've just seen your mum's car,' she said. 'We'd better get our coats.'

They fought their way back into the house and retrieved their coats, then ran down the garden towards the road. There was a huddle of people round the gate and Kelly saw Mark there, saying goodbye to everyone. His dad was with him and, as Kelly watched, she saw him look up suddenly as Mum got out of her car.

'Hey, Jen!' he shouted. Mum turned her head towards the sound, frowning, then, when she saw him, she looked startled.

At that moment, Kelly and Lizzie reached her and she focused on them.

'Hi. Had a good time?'

'Yeah, really good,' said Lizzie.

'Jen!' It was Mark's dad again, and there was something in his voice that brought Kelly up short.

But Mum put her arm firmly round Kelly's shoulders and her response was quite casual.

'Thanks for having them, Ben,' she said. 'Looks like they've had a great time.'

She seemed in a hurry to leave, and she was already getting back into the car when Mark turned to Lizzie and they hugged briefly.

Nothing passionate.

'See you next week,' he said.

'Sure,' said Lizzie. 'Thanks for a great party.'

Kelly nodded her thanks to him too and turned away embarrassed, and as she did, someone touched her arm and she swung round. It was Jack.

'Good to meet you, Kelly. Maybe we could catch up in town some time?'

Even in the dark she could sense his nervousness.

'Sure,' she said. 'That would be good.'

Why did I say that? I didn't really mean it, did I?

Five

Back home, Kelly and her mum sat together in the kitchen. Gran and Nathan had both gone to bed and the house was quiet.

Mum had made herself a hot drink and was sitting at the table, her hands round the mug, staring sightlessly towards the cooker. Kelly sat opposite her, wiping the caked black-and-white stuff from her face with Gran's special theatrical make-up remover. She threw another gunk-covered tissue in the bin.

'Yuk!'

Mum looked up. 'Make sure you get it all off before you got to bed – otherwise it'll be all over the duvet.'

'OK, OK. Doing my best.'

Mum smiled. 'It looked like a good party.'

'Umm. It was … different.'

'How?'

Kelly shrugged. 'I dunno. You sort of think Halloween's for little kids, but it kinda worked.'

'Ben had made an effort – and his kids, too.'

'Ben?'

Mum looked down at her hands. 'Ben Ryley, Mark's dad.'

Kelly frowned. 'Where's Mark's mum? I didn't see her at the party.'

Mum shrugged. 'Dunno. I don't think they're together. I ... well, we lost touch.'

'So you knew Mark's dad at college?'

'Umm. Ben was my tutor.'

'Did you go out with him, Mum?'

Her head shot up and some of her drink spilled onto the table.

'No! No of course not!'

Kelly laughed. 'Well you might have. It was ages before you met Dad, wasn't it?'

There! She'd said it. Mentioned his name.

'I'd ... I'd better go to bed.' Mum scraped back her chair, placed her mug in the sink and headed out of the kitchen. She turned back when she reached the door.

'Don't be long.'

Kelly listened to her climbing the stairs and opening her bedroom door.

It's been four years, Mum. No one could blame you.

But, even as she thought it, her heart lurched.

Kelly sat there long after every trace of the make-up had been removed, listening to the sounds of the house, the creaks as it settled for the night, the background hum coming from the electrical appliances, then the noise of a solitary car driving past the house, slowing down as it reached the sharp bend at the end of the street.

She'd only been ten when Dad left. Too young to wonder about his life before *them* – before Mum and their family. Or about Mum's life, for that matter. He was just 'Dad', Mum was just 'Mum'. But he'd been ten years older than Mum. What had happened in his life before they'd met?

She leaned back in her chair.

Who would know? Dad's parents were dead. He'd once told her that he was an afterthought, born when his mum was quite old already. And that must be true; his only brother, Uncle John, was a lot older than Dad.

Uncle John. Maybe he'd know something. Though she couldn't imagine asking him; Dad and he had never been close. Uncle John looked down on anyone less successful than him – and Dad had never been that interested in money, or the trappings that went with it.

At last she got up from her chair, yawned and stretched, then went upstairs to bed. In her room she looked at herself in the full-length mirror and smiled. The black wig and the figure-hugging black, high-necked lacey dress made her look completely different. Even though no one at the party had known about the Addams Family films, it had been a good idea.

Carefully, she took off the wig and shook out her own unruly red curls, then she reached behind her back and unhooked the dress, stepping out of it and hanging it up. She stroked it, wondering where it had come from. Had Gran worn it once? She smiled. Not for a long time; she'd certainly not be able to fit into it now.

She lay down in bed and pulled the duvet right up under her chin. But she couldn't sleep.

Alone, lying in the dark, thoughts crowded in. Dad. *Had he been there that day at the park?*

Stop it!

But what about Gran's diary, those missing pages – and the throw-away comment, '*that other business.*'

Tiny fragments, niggling pieces that didn't fit into what she'd known – about him, about his disappearance, his death.

And Dad in a fight.

It didn't fit.

She knew nothing about his past. She'd never been curious. Had he always been an artist?

And why hadn't Mum said anything about going freelance?

Stop it! Think about tonight. Think about the party.

She smiled, remembering Mark in his vampire outfit, but then frowned remembering the pretty witch all loved-up with him.

He's gorgeous, but he didn't even see me. Why should he notice me? I'm not pretty like that witchy girl and I couldn't even say two words to him, I was that shy.

Then she thought of long, gangly Jack, sitting quietly on the wall, tapping his knee in time to the music and nervously suggesting they meet up in town.

It was the first time a boy had ever asked her out – even if she didn't fancy him.

I wonder if Mark's dad fancies Mum?

It was ages before she finally slept and when she woke up she still felt tired, so she turned over and went back to sleep.

At least it was Sunday, so she didn't need to get up for school.

It seemed no time before someone was shaking her.

'Leave me alone!' she muttered, snuggling further down beneath the duvet.

'Kelly. Wake up!'

'Wozzamatter?'

She struggled to sit up. Mum was still shaking her shoulders.

'For god's sake, leave me alone,' she said, pulling herself away.

Then she saw Mum's face, pale and strained. She frowned. 'Wotisit?'

'It's Nat. I can't find him. I don't know where he is.'

Kelly rubbed her eyes and tried to focus. She looked at the clock by her bed.

'He's probably gone out. What's the panic?'

Mum sat down heavily on the edge of the bed. 'No. He wouldn't do that. It's his big tournament this morning. We have to leave in a few minutes.'

'Uh?'

'The chess tournament.' Mum got up and started to go out of the room. 'Don't you ever take any notice of what he does, Kelly? Are you so wrapped up in your own life?'

Kelly felt the tears coming. Mum never spoke to her like that.

She slid out of bed.

'It's not like him,' muttered Mum. 'He was looking forward to this chess thing. He thought he had a chance of winning it.'

Kelly tried to think. 'Have you tried his phone?'

'*Of course* I have. It keeps going to voicemail.'

'Well, when did you last see him?'

'What? Oh, I don't know. Earlier.'

'P'raps he's gone to the shops.'

'He never goes to the shops.'

Kelly blinked and stared at Mum. Why was she panicking like this? Nat was twelve years old, he wasn't a baby. What was the matter with her?

The front door slammed and Mum jumped up, clattering down the stairs.

'NAT! Where have you been?'

Kelly heard Nat mumbling and Mum's voice, anxious, high-pitched and then, a few minutes later, the sound of the car doors slamming and the engine firing up.

What the hell was that all about? She'd never seen Mum so tense. It was almost as if she'd thought Nat had been abducted or something.

Gran's voice floated up the stairs. 'Do you want your breakfast or are you going to stay in bed all day, Kelly?'

Kelly's stomach rumbled. Sunday was the one day when Gran cooked them a full English breakfast and she realised how hungry she felt. She'd been too nervous to eat much last night. She pattered along to the bathroom to wash, put on her new jeans and a baggy top, brushed her hair and ran downstairs.

Gran looked at the clock. 'Afternoon,' she said.

'Aw, c'mon Gran. It's not that late.'

'Hmm. Your breakfast's keeping warm in the oven.'

Kelly fetched it, then put it down on the kitchen table and began to eat.

'That's good, Gran. Thanks.'

'So, are you going to tell me about the party?'

Normally, Kelly would have clammed up, but she remembered all the trouble Gran had taken with the Morticia costume.

'Yeah. Really good.'

'What about your costumes?'

'Yeah, great,' she said, between mouthfuls.

'Did they know who you were supposed to be?'

Kelly hesitated. 'Mark's dad did.'

Gran sighed. 'I s'pose the youngsters hadn't seen the films.'

'It didn't matter. We looked great.'

Gran smiled.

Kelly finished her breakfast and put her empty plate in the dishwasher.

Ask her now, while she's in a good mood.

'Gran?'

'Umm.'

'Was Dad always an artist?'

The second time in twenty four hours she'd mentioned his name.

If Kelly hadn't been watching her closely, she wouldn't have noticed Gran's sharp intake of breath, covered immediately by a cough as she turned towards the sink, picked up a cloth and started wiping the table.

'Why do you ask?'

Kelly shrugged. 'Just curious.'

Gran continued to wipe the table vigorously. 'Yes,' she said slowly. 'I … I think so. I know he went to art school.'

'But he was quite old when he met Mum, wasn't he?'

Gran laughed. 'If you call thirty-five old! Now,' she continued, squeezing out the cloth and tossing it back in the sink, 'tell me about the other costumes last night. Lots of witches and vampires and skeletons, I expect.'

Kelly frowned. Gran was deliberately changing the subject.

'Yeah. All of that.'

Kelly's phone vibrated and she dragged it out of her pocket. She smiled at Lizzie's text.

'Lizzie says thanks for doing our costumes,' she said to Gran.

But that was only the last sentence.

Extra rehearsal this morning.

Mark was asking about you!!!!!!!

Kelly felt the colour rising to her cheeks.

He'd noticed her after all then? She couldn't stop smiling. She texted back.

Come round later.

She took herself off to her room to do homework, but she couldn't concentrate and kept staring out of the window. At last she shut her laptop, grabbed her coat and headed out the door.

'Where are you going?' asked Gran.

'Just getting some air. Back soon.'

She couldn't stay in the house; she wanted to run, hug herself, and she couldn't stop grinning.

He'd noticed her. Asked about her.

She was so wrapped up in her daydreams that she didn't notice where she was heading, and it wasn't until she was almost at the park gates that she came to.

Idiot. Don't go in there.

Her steps faltered, but when she looked through the gates she saw that there were lots of people about. It was another fine day and children were running around on the grass or playing on the slides or swings, and there were dog walkers, too, throwing balls or stopping to chat with other dog owners.

What harm can it do? There are loads of people here. Nothing bad can happen.

She sat on a bench, watching people enjoying themselves, in such a good mood that nothing could annoy her. The whole world was brilliant. But she felt restless, bursting with energy, and after a while she got up and started walking round the edge of the park.

She hadn't noticed that she'd reached the spot where she thought she'd seen her dad that day.

There was a shout. 'Bruno, you stupid mutt, come here.'

Kelly raised her head and focused. With a lot of barking, a large shaggy dog suddenly ran past her and lumbered into the woods, his nose to the ground and his tail wagging. Running after him, some way away, was a middle-aged couple – a man and a woman.

The woman was nearest. Puffing with effort, she shouted at Kelly. 'Can you catch him? If he gets onto a scent he'll disappear.'

Kelly ran after the dog, eventually managing to grab his collar. The couple came up.

'Thanks so much. He's an old devil.'

Kelly squatted down beside Bruno and stroked his head. The dog licked her hand, apparently not bothered about being caught and having his fun stopped.

Kelly chatted to the couple for a few minutes and then, having secured Bruno onto his lead, they walked back into the park.

Kelly followed them, dawdling. She loved the smell of the woods, the crunch of Autumn leaves beneath her feet. She stopped for a moment and took some deep breaths. And it was only then that she realised where she was.

It was right here where she thought she'd seen her dad.

Get away from here, you idiot.

But she didn't. She stood very still and looked about her, trying to conjure up that tiny glimpse she'd had of the man she thought was Dad.

And then she saw it.

No one else would have noticed it. A scrap of blue material caught on a bramble.

She stared at it.

Don't be ridiculous. Don't touch it. Walk away.

But she couldn't help herself.

She walked very slowly towards it, and with fumbling fingers pulled it away from the bramble. When she raised it to her face, she thought she caught the faintest whiff of turpentine.

Six

Kelly stuffed the scrap of material into her pocket and walked slowly out of the park. At the gates she turned to look at the gap in the trees, where the dog had crashed through.

She was right. It was at exactly the spot where she thought she'd seen Dad.

She fingered the scrap of material.

It could belong to anyone. It doesn't mean a thing.

But her mood had shifted. Slowly, she made her way home and shut herself in her room to finish her homework – though now it wasn't thoughts of Mark that distracted her.

Mum and Nat were out until the afternoon, so she and Gran sat down together for a bowl of soup at lunchtime.

'You all right, Kelly? You're very quiet.'

Kelly looked up. 'Tell me about the acting, Gran,' she said.

Gran sounded surprised. 'What? You really want to know about that?'

Kelly nodded.

Gran leant back in her chair and started to reminisce. About her time at drama college, her parts in plays round the country.

'Did you ever get to star?'

Gran laughed. 'Only in small productions. I never made the big time.'

'Why did you give it up?'

Gran shrugged. 'Once I met your granddad, it just got too hard. I didn't want to go trailing round the country any more.' She got up to put the bowls in the dishwasher. 'And Granddad was never one for the theatre.'

'It's sad you had to stop.'

Gran smiled at her. 'Not really. I did a lot of amateur stuff. And your granddad and I did other things together.'

'I never knew you were an actor, Gran. Why didn't you tell me?'

'Why should I? It was all a long time ago. And you never asked.'

No, I never asked. I've never asked about anything.

In the afternoon, Mum and Nat came back. Kelly was up in her room when she heard the car stop on the driveway and the front door open. Mum's words that morning had stung her, so she ran downstairs to greet them.

'Hi, how did you get on?'

'Rubbish,' mumbled Nat.

'He did really well to get to the final.'

Nat looked up. 'I should've won.' He shuffled off towards the kitchen.

Mum raised her eyes to the ceiling. 'He was up against much older kids. He did amazingly well to get that far.'

'You don't know anything!' shouted Nat, changing course and running up the stairs to his room, slamming his bedroom door behind him.

Mum looked upset. 'I don't know what's got into him.' She hesitated. 'P'raps I should go to him.'

'He's just upset he didn't win,' said Gran. 'I'd leave him for a bit.'

Later, Lizzie came round.

'It was good last night wasn't it?'

Kelly nodded. 'Yeah. Great.'

'That boy Jack seemed to like you.'

'What? Oh. Yeah. Well, he's OK, I s'pose.'

Lizzie frowned. 'What's the matter, Kell?'

How much can I tell her?

Slowly, Kelly started to talk, sitting on her bed, pleating and unpleating the duvet cover.

'I keep thinking about my dad,' she said quietly.

Lizzie put a hand on her arm. 'Kell, don't. Please don't go there. You were so bad when … well, when it happened. You were in a really dark place then. You don't want to go back to that, do you?'

Kelly shook her head. 'No, you don't understand, Lizzie.' She continued to fiddle with the duvet.

'What? What don't I understand?'

'There's more stuff. Not just that fight.'

'OK,' said Lizzie slowly.

So Kelly told her about the missing pages in Gran's diary, about the scrap of material in the woods.

When she'd finished talking, Lizzie looked at her. Then she squeezed her hand.

'But that ... well it doesn't *prove* anything, does it?'

Kelly didn't answer.

'You don't know why your dad got into a fight. Could have been about anything. And your gran could have cut out stuff she didn't want anyone to see. She might have said things about your dad when she was upset ... you know, stuff she regretted. And that bit of material! Honest, Kell, that's just silly. That's your imagination working overtime.'

Kelly nodded. 'I know. But still ... '

'What?'

'I just *feel* it. Things don't fit. I don't know. I can't explain.'

Lizzie stood up. 'Kell. Don't do this. You'll drive yourself mad.'

'Like I was before.'

'I didn't mean that.'

They talked of other things after that, and when Lizzie left, Kelly stood at the door and waved as she walked down the street.

She won't let me talk about it. I know she's trying to protect me, but if can't tell Lizzie, who can I tell?

I can't leave it, Lizzie.

It was late before she finished her homework, but when she finally crawled into bed, again she couldn't sleep. Although she was bone-tired, things kept whirling around in her head, and when she shut her eyes the faint smell of turpentine was still there, filling her nostrils, mocking her.

She got out of bed and padded over to the window. She drew the curtains back a little way and stared out at the front garden. There was a carpet of fallen leaves on the lawn, but it was a still night and there'd be no more blown down just yet. The moon had risen and its pale light illuminated the trees and flower bed, making their shapes ghostly and unrecognisable.

She was just about to turn back when something moved in the tall hedge at the end of the garden. Kelly's heart started pounding and she stared out, biting her lip, but she couldn't see anything.

Is there someone watching us. Watching me?

She shivered and quickly drew back from the window and, if she'd not been fully alert, she wouldn't have heard the noise, a sudden sob, quickly stifled, coming from Nathan's room.

She listened for a few moments and then there was another.

She grabbed a torch from beside her bed and tiptoed quietly along the passage. For a few moments she stood, irresolute, outside his door.

Will he want me to know he's been crying? That chess thing must have really upset him. P'raps it's best if I go away.

She had almost decided to go back when she heard another sob. She hesitated and then, remembering Mum's words, 'You never take any notice of what he does,' she reached for the door handle and walked into his room.

He was sitting up in bed and he jumped when she came in, blinking as she shone the torch at him.

'Nat,' she began.

'Go away,' he hissed at her, wiping his eyes with the back of his hand.

'I … I'm really sorry about the chess.'

'Go away!' he said, louder this time.

'OK, OK. But … '

He lay down and turned his back to her, and it was then that the beam of her torch caught a glint of something. Something he was clutching to his chest.

It was the photo. The photo of him and Dad that he kept on the table by his bed.

She felt the tears prick behind her eyes. 'Oh Nat,' she said softly. 'I miss him, too. I miss him all the time.'

Nat didn't answer, and after a while she left him, closing the door softly behind her.

Back in her room she sat on her bed, the torch loose in her hands.

Nat had only been eight when Dad had left them. She'd thought, somehow, that he was too young to remember. That he'd been too young for it to affect him.

Stupid! Of course he remembers. Yet he'd seemed to cope OK when Dad went. It wasn't Nat who'd had the breakdown, then all those hours of therapy. He'd just soldiered on. All the attention had been on her.

At breakfast the next morning, Nat was late down.

Kelly put a hand on his shoulder. 'You OK?' she whispered, when Mum and Gran were out of earshot, but he shrugged her off and refused to answer.

At school, she could feel Lizzie watching her and at one point Kelly turned to her, laughing.

'Will you stop it!'

'What?'

'Stop looking at me as if I'm going to break down any minute.'

Lizzie bit her lip. 'Sorry, Kell. I didn't mean to, but ... you know, the way you were yesterday, I was worried about you.'

'Well don't be. You're right. My imagination's been getting out of hand. Forget what I said.'

Lizzie looked relieved. 'You sure you're OK?'

'Sure.'

They parted then, to go to separate lessons. As Kelly was making her way down the corridor to the art room, she saw Jack coming in the opposite direction. He was impossible to miss, with his shambling gait, towering over all the kids around him. He stopped when he reached her.

'Hi.'

'Hi, Jack.' She smiled at him. He was no threat. She didn't fancy him, but he was nice. She'd liked the way he'd spoken to her at the party.

'You OK?' He was already blushing, shifting his feet from side to side.

She nodded. 'Fine.'

Other pupils were surging past him. She could see he was trying to say something.

'D'you fancy grabbing a coffee in town at the weekend?' he blurted out at last.

'Sure. Where?'

He quickly named a place and a time. It sounded as though he'd been rehearsing it.

'OK. See you then.'

'Great,' he said, suddenly smiling.

She looked at the time. She was already late. 'Better get on,' she said.

'Me too.'

Kelly loved art lessons. She knew she wasn't anywhere near as good as her Dad, but she was still one of the best in the class and she was always able to lose herself in the work. Halfway through the lesson, the teacher asked for volunteers to paint scenery for the production of Romeo and Juliet, and Kelly immediately put up her hand.

'You'll have to do a lot of it in your spare time,' said her teacher.

'Will we be working in the school theatre?' asked Kelly.

'Yes. We'll have to sketch in the background on the big backdrops, then there'll be a lot of painting to do.'

'Sounds good.'

One of her friends leant towards her and whispered, 'I know what you're up to, Kelly Wilson. You just want to ogle Mark Ryley.'

'I do NOT.'

'You SO do! Not saying I blame you or anything – he's drop-dead gorgeous.'

Kelly laughed.

Later, when she was walking home with Lizzie, she told her about painting the scenery for the play.

'Hey, that's great. You'll do a brilliant job.'

'And maybe I'll get to see you snog Mark!'

Lizzie punched her lightly on the arm. 'Will you stop that! Anyway, he's spoken for.'

'What? That soppy witch girl?'

Lizzie nodded. 'Think so. She's always hanging round.'

'Is she in the drama group?'

'Yeah. She's rubbish at acting though.'

'So why's she … '

Lizzie shrugged. 'Looks good in the crowd scenes, I suppose!'

They both laughed, then Kelly said, 'Hey, I've got a date!'

'What?' Lizzie stopped in her tracks. 'Now you tell me.'

Kelly grinned. 'It's only with that guy at the party, Jack. I'm going to have a coffee with him in town at the weekend.'

'Coffee, eh?'

Kelly raised her eyes to the sky. 'Honestly, Lizzie, I don't fancy him one bit, but … well, he was easy to talk to.'

'Don't break his heart, girl. I could see he fancies you!'

'Nah!'

'He does, he fancies you rotten.'

They parted at Lizzie's door and Kelly walked on up the street. At home, she shut herself in her bedroom and took out her school books. But she didn't open them. Instead, she stared out of the window.

What was Dad doing before he met Mum?

She knew the art school he'd gone to – Gran had

mentioned it the other night – so she googled it and went into the list of previous pupils. She typed in his name.

It came up. She frowned when she saw the dates. He'd been there three years, and he was there when he and Mum had married.

What about before then?

Seven

Kelly widened the search, but all that came up for Steve Wilson was about his disappearance and apparent suicide, and she couldn't bear to trawl through all that again.

There was no mention of the fight in the pub.

Eventually she gave up and went downstairs to watch television, but Nathan was there, glued to some noisy programme involving a lot of shooting. He looked up when she came in and scowled.

'I was here first.'

'OK. OK.'

'If you want to watch something you can see it online.'

Kelly bit back an angry response, remembering, just in time, the tearful Nat of last night.

'No. I'm not that bothered.'

She sat down beside him on the couch, grabbed a

cushion and hugged it to herself. Nat squirmed and then, sighing, switched off the telly. He got up, put his hands in his pockets and stared at the floor. He started to move off towards the door.

'Don't go, Nat.'

'Doesn't matter. It was a rubbish film,' he muttered.

'Nat.'

'Wot?'

She took a quick breath. 'Do you ever think about Dad?'

Nat didn't raise his head. 'Sometimes,' he said, so quietly she could hardly hear him.

'I still think about him a lot,' said Kelly. 'Sometimes … sometimes I think I can feel him around.'

'Don't be STUPID! Nat was flushed now, angry. He hurried out of the room, slamming the door behind him.

He's still raw. Why didn't I realise? It must be hard for him, surrounded by women. But he's not going to talk about it.

During the next few days Kelly trawled the internet, trying to find out more about her dad that didn't involve his disappearance, but she got nowhere.

It was as if he'd not existed before going to art college. Where did he go to school? Or uni? She was fairly sure he had been to uni. Did he have old friends who'd known him then?

She tried to think back to the time he'd gone. So many people had been in and out of the house. Were some of them friends from way back? Maybe Mum knew more.

She tried asking her. 'Mum, what did Dad do before he went to Art College?'

Mum was peeling some vegetables at the sink, her back to Kelly, and she tensed briefly before turning round.

'Why are you suddenly asking about Dad,' she said quietly. 'You're not getting all stressed again are you?'

Kelly shook her head. 'I'd just like to know,' she said.

Mum sat down opposite her. 'He never talked about what he'd done before art college,' she said slowly. 'He said his parents made him go to uni, but he hated the course. I got the impression that he'd not done a lot, hadn't really found his way until he started at college. He never said much about his life before we met.'

'So you don't even know where he went to school?'

'School? Oh, yes, it was some big comprehensive in London.'

'So, his family lived in London?'

'Yes. I think so.'

'But surely you must know! You met his mum and dad – and Uncle John.'

She shook her head. 'No, I never knew his parents. They'd died before I met Dad.'

Kelly was quiet for a while. 'I s'pose Uncle John would know what Dad did.'

'I suppose so. Though they didn't talk much. They were so ... so different.'

Oh well. P'raps I could ask Uncle John. But Christmas is weeks away.

The next afternoon, Kelly went back to the library, looking through their newspaper archives again in case she'd missed something.

Same old, same old.

But there was one thing that wasn't the same. She tried to access the old newspaper report of Dad's fight outside the pub, but she couldn't find it. The newspaper for that day didn't seem to be there any more.

Once she'd put in the code the librarian had given her, it had been easy enough to find it last time.

Kelly frowned at the screen, then went over to the librarian and asked for help, but the librarian couldn't find that day's newspaper either.

'Technology, eh?' she said, finally giving up. 'It'll be there somewhere.'

'Doesn't matter,' said Kelly.

But it did matter.

She couldn't help feeling that this man Dad had fought with was somehow important. And now, she couldn't even find a record of the fight. Why wasn't it there?

It was almost as if someone was trying to make sure she didn't find out anything she shouldn't. She thought again of that slight movement in the hedge on that moonlit night, and shivered.

She was so absorbed in her thoughts about Dad that she'd almost forgotten about meeting Jack in town on Saturday.

She didn't take any special care (after all, it wasn't as if he was a *boyfriend* or anything), but she did wear clean jeans and pulled her hair back into a ponytail.

He was waiting when she arrived at the café. It wasn't where her friends hung out and she was grateful he'd suggested somewhere different, where they wouldn't be on view to a load of people from school.

She waved at him as she came into the café and Jack jumped up, knocking into someone's chair.

She smiled and sat down. 'It's nice here,' she said.

He made a face. 'It's full of oldies,' he said. 'It's just I thought … '

'Better not be stared at by a load of our school friends,' she finished.

'Yeah. Something like that.'

'I'm glad.'

Once they'd ordered coffees the conversation was stilted. They talked a bit about the party and who'd been there, then they sat silent.

'What are you going to do when you leave school,' said Jack, then, seeing her raise an eyebrow, he blushed again. 'Sorry, that was so crass. I sound like your grandad or someone.'

She laughed. 'It's OK.' She looked down into her cup, frowning. 'I dunno. I'm not much good at anything – except art.'

'So will you try for art college?'

Dad again, invading her thoughts.

Then, quite unexpectedly, she felt tears coming to her eyes. She brushed them away angrily and took a gulp of coffee, but it was too hot and she spluttered, her eyes streaming now.

She grabbed a napkin and blew her nose. 'Sorry. Coffee was a bit hot.'

But he'd noticed.

'Your dad was an artist, wasn't he?'

How does he know that? But everyone knew. Anyone who was around four years ago would have known. The papers had been full of it. A big story for a small town.

'Yeah.' She didn't meet his eyes.

'I'm so sorry, Kelly. I didn't mean to … '

'Doesn't matter. It's all in the past.' She sniffed. 'So, what do *you* want to be when you grow up?'

'I deserved that!' He smiled, looking more relaxed.

'Well?'

'Me? I'd like to be a journalist.'

'A journalist!' She remembered them all sniffing around the house, trying to get pictures of the family. She shuddered.

'Why a journalist? Invading people's lives and stuff.'

He looked at her. 'No, Kelly, not that sort. Not an investigative journo. Feature writing, that sort of thing.'

Her shoulders untensed. 'Oh, that's different, is it?'

'Yep. No doorstepping. Nothing like that.'

She didn't reply.

'I like writing,' he said lamely. 'And, well, my dad's a journalist, so I suppose it's in the genes.'

His dad. Maybe he was one of the ones there, four years ago.

Jack seemed to read her thoughts.

'My dad was on the local paper when your dad died,' he said quietly. 'But he wouldn't have been camping out on your doorstep.'

'Who said my dad died?' she blurted out. 'No one ever found his body.'

Why did I say that?

Jack looked shocked. 'Kelly, I'm really sorry. I didn't mean to upset you. I'm an idiot.'

'No. I'm the idiot,' said Kelly. 'It's just … I dunno. Some weird things have happened.'

Her coffee had spilled a little on the wooden table and she pushed the liquid around with her finger, spreading it further.

She could feel Jack's eyes on her. 'D'you want to tell me about it?'

Kelly shrugged. 'It's not important,' she said.

'Sounds as though it's important to you.'

Finally she raised her eyes and looked at him. 'You don't want to know, Jack. It's probably all in my head.' She paused. 'Lizzie thinks I'm going mad again.'

'Is that what you think?'

'I don't know,' she said quietly. 'But it scares me.'

'If you tell me what's been happening,' said Jack, 'I swear I won't say a thing to anyone.'

Kelly bit her lip. 'Really? You swear?'

He nodded.

'And you won't think I'm nuts?'

Jack smiled. 'Promise.'

Can I trust him? I hardly know him. But maybe it would be good to talk about it with him. Someone who's not involved.

And then, suddenly, she couldn't stop talking. It all came out, words tumbling over themselves, everything out of sequence. And all the time she was speaking, Jack kept quiet.

When she'd finished, she took a deep breath and looked across at him.

'It sounds mad, doesn't it?'

Jack shook his head. 'No,' he said after a pause. 'Not all of it.'

'What d'you mean?'

'Well,' he said slowly, choosing his words carefully, 'if it had just been a *feeling* – you know, when you thought you'd seen your dad, and imagining that there was someone in your garden, well that could have been all in your head.'

'But?'

'But the pages from your gran's diary going missing, then the archive report disappearing from the library records – that's real enough. And your mum saying nothing about going freelance.'

Kelly interrupted him. 'I don't think that's got anything to do with it. She just forgot to tell us. And, to be fair, I've never taken any interest in what she does.'

'So, what does she do – exactly?'

Kelly laughed. 'She's a software engineer. I know it sounds mad, but I don't really know what that means. I guess she writes programs for computers and fixes them when they go wrong. Something like that. Anyway, she's a whizz with technology.'

'A whizz with technology?'

Kelly frowned. 'You don't think she could have removed that archive report, do you?'

'It's possible, I suppose, but she'd have to have access to all the library passwords to do that.'

'Yeah. And they change them every day. I was given a different one every time I went.'

'Did she know you'd been looking up about the fight?'

Kelly shook her head. 'No. No one knew. Only Lizzie.'

'Lizzie's a good friend to you, isn't she?'

Kelly nodded. 'The best.' She hesitated and then went on quietly. 'She was with me all through ... all through that bad time.'

'When your dad disappeared?'

'Yeah. She'd come round every day, even when I was at my maddest, even when I was rotten to her, she never let me down. She always stuck by me.'

'And she was, what – only ten?'

Kelly smiled. 'Only a kid. She could easily have given up on me. I wouldn't have blamed her. Then, when I went back to school, she was always there for me. A lot of the others didn't know what to say, so they avoided me, made me feel a bit of a freak.' She hesitated. 'Well, I guess I was.'

'You'd gone through something they couldn't even imagine.'

'Yeah. I s'pose.'

They were silent for a few moments, then Jack leant back in his chair and clasped his hands behind his head.

'And your dad's background. That's a bit of a mystery.'

'It's probably nothing. I expect I can find out easily enough what he did before he went to art college, but it was weird that Mum didn't seem to know.'

'*Seem* to … ?'

'I don't think she was lying. I really don't think she knew.'

'Umm.'

'What?'

'You're right. There are gaps – and bits that don't fit.'

For the first time, Kelly's shoulders dropped. 'Thanks for believing me,' she muttered.

Jack looked across the table at her, meeting her eyes. 'Do you … would you like me to help you? I mean, if you want to go on with this?'

Someone helping me. Is that what I want?

'I dunno. There's not a lot more I can do. Every time I try and find out more, I reach a dead end.'

'Well, I could ask my dad.'

'What!!'

'No,' he said quickly, 'I don't mean tell him about your dad and these bits that don't fit. I mean, I could ask him about sources and stuff.'

'Sources?'

'Yeah.' Jack leant forward. 'Look, I could say I was doing something for school, trying to find out about working as a journalist, what sources to go to. All that sort of stuff.'

She frowned. 'Would he help?'

''Course he'd help.'

'Well,' she said, 'I suppose … '

Jack tipped his chair back towards the table and leant forwards. He took her hands in his. It seemed a completely natural gesture and Kelly didn't try to pull away.

'Look,' he said, 'You shouldn't be carrying all this stuff on your own. Two heads are better than one and all that. I'd like to help.'

'It's probably nothing.'

'Doesn't sound like nothing to me.'

Suddenly, Jack's phone vibrated and he dragged it out of his pocket.

'Hey. I've gotta go, Kelly. Sorry. I'm due at the cycling club in ten minutes.'

They both stood up, banging into each other and then springing apart.

'You won't say anything to anyone at school?'

Jack smiled. 'Of course I won't.'

He leant forward and gave her an awkward hug. 'See you soon. I'll let you know what I can find out.'

She hugged him back, then, as she watched him lope out of the door and run down the street, she frowned.

I shouldn't have hugged him. It'll give him ideas. I absolutely DO NOT fancy him.

But it would be SO good to be able to talk to someone who believed her, someone who didn't think she was a complete mad person.

Neither of them had noticed the man who had come into the café just after them and sat in the far corner with his back to them. Not long after Kelly went out the door, he got up and left the café, speaking into his phone as he walked quickly down the street.

Eight

Kelly made her way home, chewing her lip and frowning.

What was I thinking?

What had she done, telling Jack all that? Telling a stranger all that personal stuff about Dad.

What if he started poking about, trying to find scandal, just like those horrible journalists who'd never left them alone when Dad disappeared? She didn't remember much, but she could still see the surging crowd of cameras coming towards them whenever they left the house. Horrible, horrible.

She couldn't tell Mum or Gran what she'd done. They'd be really upset if they thought she'd been talking to Jack about Dad.

And Lizzie. She'd never kept stuff from Lizzie. Lizzie had always known everything about her.

On cue, her phone rang. It was Lizzie. Kelly swallowed. No point putting it off. She'd have to talk to her soon.

'Hi!'

'Well?'

'Well what?'

'Duh! Your date with Jack! How did it go?'

'Yeah. It was good. He's really nice.'

'Did you have a little snog when you said goodbye?'

Kelly flushed as she thought of that brief hug.

'No of course not! I told you, I don't fancy him.'

'Not just a little bit?'

Kelly laughed. 'Not even a little bit.'

They arranged to meet up later and, for the first time ever, Kelly dreaded seeing Lizzie. She'd know Kelly was keeping something from her.

Damn. What have I started?

But it had been good to talk it through with Jack.

She walked past the park gates without glancing in, but she fingered the scrap of material which was still in her pocket and, just for a few moments, she allowed herself to fantasise. Just suppose Dad wasn't dead, that instead he'd pulled off some elaborate hoax. But why? What possible reason could he have?

Was he wanted for some crime?

Did he have another family somewhere?

Then she started to laugh. They were ridiculous reasons. Her dad, the vague, gentle artist, having another life as a gangster or keeping a secret family and deceiving Mum. There was no way he'd be able to do any of that!

P'raps Jack really will be able to find out more. He'll be better at it than me. He won't have the baggage.

When she reached the house, Kelly took off her coat and hung it in the hall.

'Hello, Kelly.'

'Hi, Gran.' Kelly walked through into the lounge where her gran was sitting, staring at some old photo albums.

'What are those?'

Gran looked up. 'You know you were asking about my acting days?'

'Umm.'

'Well, I thought you might like to see some of these. They were at the bottom of that case, with my acting clothes. I'd forgotten all about them.'

Kelly sat down beside her. 'Hey, are these photos of the productions you were in?'

Gran nodded. 'Can you pick me out?'

Kelly looked more closely at the row of people taking a bow on some stage.

She pointed. 'That's never you!'

Gran smiled. 'I wasn't bad looking then.'

Kelly sat back. 'Not bad looking. You were a knockout, Gran!'

She couldn't believe it. Gran must have been, what, in her early twenties – before Mum came along, anyway – and she looked stunning.

Gran smiled. 'It's amazing what lighting and make-up can do,' she said.

Kelly was taken aback. This had obviously been such a big part of Gran's life. Why had she never known about it?

'Lizzie's coming round later, Gran. Can I show her these? You know she's in the drama club at school. She'd be well impressed.'

'Yes, if you like. If you think she'd be interested.' Gran

heaved herself up off the sofa. 'You'd never wanted to act then, Kelly?'

'Me? No, I'm rubbish at it.'

Kelly watched as Gran went out of the room and headed into the kitchen.

She's being really nice to me at the moment. She hasn't snapped at me for at least a week. Must be a record.

Kelly smiled to herself and went on leafing through the old photos. Looking through these might stop Lizzie asking too many questions.

She fetched a magnifying glass so she could see them better, look at Gran in her glamorous days. The albums spanned three or four years, all annotated – Brighton, Cambridge, Lincoln and other towns, with many of the same faces appearing again and again.

She must have been with some touring company.

They all looked so young!

When Lizzie came round later, Kelly showed her the albums and she pored over them with Gran, asking questions about the productions – what the plays were, where the theatres were, what role Gran had played.

'Goodness, Lizzie,' said Gran, laughing. 'What an inquisition. It's such a long time ago I really can't remember much.'

Lizzie sat back, hugging one of the albums to her. 'It must have been great,' she sighed. 'Going on tour, acting every night.'

'Umm,' said Gran. 'It's not that glamorous, Lizzie. It's really hard work.'

'But you loved it?'

Gran said nothing for a moment, then quietly, 'Yes. Yes I did.'

After tea, Lizzie and Kelly went up to Kelly's room.

'Now,' said Lizzie. 'Tell.'

Kelly grinned. 'Honest, there's nothing to tell. We had coffee, we talked, then he went off to his cycle club.'

'*Cycle* club!'

'Yeah. I know! Mark is a member, too.'

'Mark! I can't believe it! That's weird.'

'What?'

'I just can't see him in lycra, helmet, head down, muscles rippling, pedaling away.'

'I can!'

Lizzie laughed. 'You don't give up, do you? He's off limits, Kell. He's all loved-up with his little witchy girlfriend. Honestly, you should see them together.' She put her finger in her mouth and gave a gagging sound.

Kelly put her hands over her ears, laughing. 'I don't want to know!'

Lizzie nudged her. 'Hey, it's good to see you laughing.'

Kelly sniffed. 'Sorry. I know I've been a bit tense. Anyway, how's the play going?'

'Yeah. It's OK. Usual stuff, people forgetting their lines, forgetting their moves, cracking up when they shouldn't, the drama teacher getting stressed.'

'We'll be starting on the sets soon,' said Kelly. 'We'll probably be in the hall some of the time you're rehearsing.'

'Then you'll be able to lust after Mark from close quarters!'

'I wish!'

'He's a good actor, though, I'll give him that. He's a convincing Romeo.'

'What, you mean he looks as though he's really in love with you?'

Lizzie laughed. 'Yeah. He really throws himself into it.'

'Bet the witch hates that!'

'Sometimes I catch her looking at us, so I really pile on the passion!'

'Can't wait to see that.'

'Umm. Anyway, tell me more about Jack.'

'Nothing to tell. He's a good bloke. He listens. He's easy to talk to.'

'So, what did you talk about.'

Kelly looked away. 'Oh this and that. School … friends … that sort of stuff.'

'Not the cycling club then?'

'As if!'

'And you really don't fancy him?'

'NO! How many times!' She paused. 'But he could be a good friend.'

Lizzie raised an eyebrow.

'He could Lizzie. Not … not like you, obviously. But … well he's the sort of guy you can trust.'

'Umm. Careful, Kell. You don't want to trust boys with your secrets.'

Kelly felt the colour rise to her cheeks, but Lizzie didn't notice – she was too busy talking about some girl who had confided something to a bloke and then the next day it was all round the school.

That won't happen. Jack's not the sort of bloke to gossip. I'm sure he's not.

Kelly was relieved when Lizzie went home. It had felt strange not telling her the whole truth about Jack. She'd never kept anything from her before.

But it's not as if I lied to her or anything.

That night, Kelly woke up suddenly. She got out of bed and pattered over to the window. There was no moon – it was a dull damp, cloudy night, but she noticed there was light coming from the kitchen window, shining out onto the garden.

Mum must still be up. I'll go down and get myself a drink.

She walked quietly down the stairs and along the hallway to the kitchen. The door was ajar and she heard the sound of voices.

So not just Mum. Gran must still be up. That's not like her …

She was just about to go into the kitchen when something made her hesitate. Something in the way Mum and Gran were talking.

Kelly stood very still and listened.

'Have you noticed?' said Gran. 'Kelly's started talking about Steve again.'

'Umm. But maybe it's a good thing. If she can mention him without getting upset.'

'I don't know. It worries me. Remember how she was when he went.'

Kelly heard Gran's chair shift and she could see through the half-open door that she'd moved closer to Mum and had her hand on her arm.

'You've got to keep strong, love, for her – and for Nat.'

And then the sounds of Mum crying, of Gran comforting her.

After a while Mum sniffed and Kelly heard her blowing her nose. 'But you said, after a few years, maybe … That's why I went freelance. In case … you know.'

Then Gran's voice, firm, definite. 'I was wrong. I don't think that's going to happen. You've got to accept it, love.'

'Then why did you say it? Why did you even suggest it?' Mum's voice was angry and Kelly saw her scrape her chair back and stand up.

'How *could* you? How could you do that?'

Gran's voice was quiet. She had risen to her feet, too, and she was pacing up and down. Kelly couldn't catch everything she said, just the odd word. 'Breakdown … under a lot of strain … sometimes … '

Kelly stood there outside the door, her fists clenched, holding her breath.

What are they talking about? Is Gran saying she thought Dad might not have died? Why would she say that? Has Mum been hanging on to some little thread of hope all this time?

Her first instinct was to rush in and confront them, and her hand was on the door handle when she saw Mum lurch across the room towards Gran's open arms.

She watched as they hugged and she heard Mum let out a keening cry as she sobbed onto Gran's shoulder. Gran's head was turned towards Kelly. Her eyes were dry and her expression gave nothing away.

The word *actor* floated into Kelly's brain and she couldn't shift it.

For a few moments longer she stayed where she was, then

she crept back up the stairs to bed. It wasn't until she got to her room that she noticed that her nails had made deep imprints in the palms of her hands.

Nine

Kelly didn't sleep for ages, confused thoughts whirling around in her head, and when she did at last fall asleep, not long before dawn, she had a horrible nightmare about Dad walking into the sea, swimming strongly at first, but then gradually disappearing beneath waves which grew bigger and bigger, crashing down on his head and eventually swallowing him.

She knew she looked dreadful the next morning. Both Gran and Mum asked her if she was all right, and she was glad she had an excuse to escape; she had volunteered to go the school and help start painting the scenery for the play. She was a bit early and the school was still locked up, but soon the art teacher arrived, together with a gaggle of other students.

'Thanks everyone,' said the teacher as she unlocked the door. 'I've roughed out the flats; it's just a question of talking about colours and who's going to do what.'

It was strange to be in the school when there was nobody about. In the art room, the flats were stacked against the wall, and when the art teacher pulled them all out it was already obvious which were going to be in various scenes. There was a balcony and some buildings for the town scenes, which could then be converted into the tomb and the friar's cell.

'Kelly, could you make a start on the trees and vegetation on this one?' said the art teacher.

Kelly didn't answer, the strange scene from last night still playing over and over in her head.

'Kelly?'

She started. 'Sorry. What?'

The art teacher repeated her question and Kelly nodded.

The other helpers left at lunchtime, but Kelly couldn't face going home, so she volunteered to stay into the afternoon. She and her teacher had a break and shared some sandwiches and chatted about the technical difficulties of painting scenery.

'When will we be taking them to the drama club?' asked Kelly.

'Some time next week,' said her teacher. 'There are just a few more to do, then when they're all dry we'll put them in place in the theatre and see how they look.'

They worked on together for another hour or so, then her teacher said she had to go. They packed up the paints and took off their overalls and washed their hands. Just as they were leaving, her teacher said, 'Have you thought any more about art college, Kelly?

Kelly shrugged. 'I've thought about it but … I dunno. I'm not sure I'd be good enough to make a career of it.'

'Well, there's plenty of time. But *I* think you'd certainly be good enough.'

Following Dad. But I'd never be as good as him.

The next day, on the way to school, Kelly told Lizzie all about the scenery for the play.

'It's gonna look great!' she said.

'Can't wait to see it. We had another rehearsal yesterday.'

'Yeah? How's it going?'

'Coming together.' She grinned. 'Hey, the witch and Mark had a mega row!'

'No way!'

Lizzie nodded. 'I heard it. I was in the toilet and they were talking in the passage outside.'

'What about?'

'Usual thing. Him being too passionate as Romeo!'

'Isn't that the point of the play?'

Lizzie laughed. 'Of course it is! But try telling the witch that!'

'What did Mark say?'

'I couldn't hear much, but he was getting pretty pissed off with her. Hey, maybe he'll ditch her and then you'll be in with a chance.'

Kelly smiled. 'Nah. He's more likely to fall for you!'

At lunchtime, they walked together round the school yard. It was a cold day but bright and sunny and, as Kelly squinted up at the sky, she noticed how the bare branches of the trees surrounding the school made intricate patterns against the brightness of the sky. Dad would have captured those patterns on canvas.

'Kelly!' Someone was calling her name and she stopped walking and turned round. Jack was waving at her and running towards her.

'Uh-huh,' said Lizzie, 'Here comes lover-boy.'

'He is NOT.'

Jack caught them up. 'Hi. Er … Kelly, can I have a word?'

Lizzie raised her eyebrows and walked on. Kelly looked after her, embarrassed.

'What's the matter?'

Jack bent over, his hands on his knees, still puffing. 'I did a bit of research at the weekend,' he said quietly.

Suddenly Kelly was all ears. 'Did you find something?'

'I dunno. It may be nothing.' He looked round. 'Let's walk over there.'

They set off towards the far end of the yard, where there were no other kids around.

'What?' she said, as soon as they were out of earshot.

'Well, it may be nothing.'

'You said that … but?'

'But.' He looked at the ground. 'I hope you don't mind, but I asked my dad about the case.'

'The case. My dad's disappearance was a *case*?!'

'Well. Yeah.'

'Sorry. I s'pose that's what they'd call it.' She hesitated. 'You didn't say you'd been talking to me about it?'

Jack shook his head. 'Like I said, I told him it was a project about how journalists research stuff, their sources. And ... I sort of slipped in your dad's disappearance as an example of something he'd worked on – something local.'

'So?" Kelly's heart began to beat a little more quickly.

'He said he remembered it well and that it was an odd one.'

'An *odd* one. What does that mean?'

'He said he'd given up trying to research your dad's background because every time he tried, he came up against a blank wall.'

Kelly stared at him. 'He said *that*?'

Jack nodded. 'And there's more.'

'Yeah?'

'I ... well, I mentioned the fight outside the pub. Said I'd been doing a bit of my own research and I'd seen something about it.'

'What did he say?'

'He was gobsmacked. Said he'd heard nothing about that and where was my source.' Jack looked down at his feet. 'I said it was in a back copy of the local paper at the library, like you told me.'

'And did you tell him that it's disappeared. The record's disappeared?'

'You don't know that, Kelly. If you found it once, it'll be there somewhere.'

Kelly shook her head. 'I dunno. I get the feeling someone's got rid of it.'

'But how could they?'

'I haven't a clue. But it's all electronic, isn't it? It would be easy enough to wipe.'

'Like your dad's early life,' he said quietly.

Kelly stared at him. 'You really think that?'

Jack met her eyes. 'Something's odd about this,' he said. 'These days, when everything's out there, when our whole lives are online, there are these gaps in your dad's life.'

'So, you believe me?'

'Absolutely.' He put his hand through his hair. 'Kelly, do you want me to go on digging? It could … well, it could be upsetting. We might find out stuff you'd rather not know.'

'I want to know,' she said quietly. 'Whatever it is.'

The bell went for the end of lunch and they turned and walked back into school together.

'I'll be in touch.'

'OK.'

'And don't leave messages on my phone about this.'

She stared at him. 'What! Why ever not?'

'I dunno. I just have this feeling … ' He didn't meet her eyes but looked into the distance, frowning. 'I think it's best to be careful.'

Kelly felt a lurch of fear in her gut. 'OK,' she said slowly. Then she grinned. 'Like we're in some really bad TV drama!'

Jack said nothing and they parted at the entrance to the school.

Straight away, Lizzie came up to Kelly. 'What were you talking about? It all looked a bit heavy.'

Kelly smiled and ran her hand through her curls, unconsciously mimicking Jack's gesture. 'Nothing much.'

'Didn't look like nothing much.'

Kelly shrugged. 'He was just telling me about a project he's doing – for school.'

Lizzie put her hand to her mouth. 'Boring!' Then she went on. 'Everyone's already saying you two are an item!'

'What?'

'You know what this place is like.'

'Well, we're NOT. And we're never gonna be.'

'OK, OK, whatever.'

All through the next lesson, Kelly found it impossible to concentrate. Did they really think she and Jack were an item? That was seriously embarrassing. They'd have to make sure they met away from school in future. She gazed out of the window onto the school yard. It was strange that Jack's dad knew nothing of the fight outside the pub, but then, at the time, it hadn't been a big deal. Two blokes coming out of a pub and having a go at each other. Hardly headline news. It was only when it was lined up with Dad's disappearance, an indication that something was not right, perhaps that he was in some sort of trouble, that there might have been a reason for him taking his life.

Surely the reporters would have been looking for reasons – for some scandal about him – so why had no one spotted that? And why couldn't she find the article again? She hadn't imagined it, had she? She wasn't going nuts again.

'Kelly Wilson!'

She came back to earth to find the maths teacher pointing his finger at her accusingly.

She jumped. 'Sorry, what did you say?'

'I *knew* you weren't listening.' He repeated his question. She blushed and tried to focus.

In the following lesson, the school secretary opened the classroom door and came in. She whispered something to the teacher.

'Kelly,' said the teacher quietly.

'Yes?'

The teacher cleared her throat. 'Can you go and see the head, please.'

Kelly frowned. Surely, not concentrating in a maths lesson wasn't such a crime? Not bad enough to be summoned to the head's office. Slowly she got up and followed the school secretary out of the room and down the corridor.

'What's this about?' asked Kelly.

The secretary looked at her kindly. 'It's all right, dear,' she said. 'You've done nothing wrong.'

That's something. Maybe I've done something right for a change. Maybe she wants to say thank you for giving up my Sunday to paint the scenery for the play.

But nothing prepared her for the scene when she went into the head's office. Mum was standing by the head's desk. Nathan was with her and Mum had her arm round his shoulders. Her face was ashen and suddenly she looked much older.

Kelly didn't even notice the presence of the head. 'Mum! What's happened? What is it? Is it Gran? Is she … ?'

Mum shook her head. 'No darling,' she said, 'Gran's fine.'

Darling! She never calls me darling!

Kelly saw Mum's hand tighten on Nat's shoulder. 'Kelly, we've had some news … about Dad.'

For a moment, Kelly's heart soared.

They've found him. He's had amnesia or something. He's alive! I knew it!

'The police have just been round. Some … ' she hesitated,

then licked her lips and continued, her voice beginning to break. 'They've found some remains.'

Kelly couldn't move. She wanted to walk into Mum's arms and be hugged, but if she did that she knew she'd break down.

'What? And they think it's Dad?' she whispered.

Mum nodded silently, then she moved forward and enfolded Kelly so that all three of them, Kelly, Mum and Nat, were encircled. Mum was crying and so was Nat, but Kelly was numb. She found she couldn't react. She disentangled herself.

'You mean they don't know. They just suspect it's him?' Then her brain engaged. 'But surely, if he drowned … ' She forced herself to go on. 'Surely, there'd be nothing … nothing left by now.'

Mum nodded again and she cleared her throat. 'The … remains were found in a cave apparently. Not far from where his clothes were left. The police said the cave was well-hidden … but they're pretty sure it's him. They'll do … you know, forensic tests … '

The head stood up. 'I'm so very sorry,' she said. Then added. 'Your mum's come to take you home.'

Mum cleared her throat. 'I think it's best. Can you get your things?'

Kelly nodded.

'Don't worry about that,' said the head. 'My secretary's gone to get them.'

They walked to the car in silence, Mum's arm still round Nat's shoulders. She slipped her free hand into Kelly's.

Kelly got in the front seat and put on her seat belt. Nat sat in the back and she could hear him sniffing.

'I wanted to tell you myself,' said Mum. 'In case it's on the news or anything.' She stabbed the keys in the ignition, but couldn't seem to turn them.

'Damn!' Then she leant over the steering wheel and sobbed.

'Mum!' Kelly stretched over and put her hand on her knee.

'I don't know why I'm crying,' said Mum, wiping her nose with a tissue. 'I've known all along – in my heart.'

'Is it … ? Are they quite sure?'

'Well, yes. Yes. 90 percent.'

Kelly sat very still, staring out into the road as Mum drove jerkily home. Once she had to swerve hard to avoid a cyclist.

'Mum!'

'Sorry,' she mumbled, and Kelly could see the shock in her face.

When they got back to the house, Gran was there.

'I've boiled the kettle,' she said.

She made them all sit down. 'Sweet tea. Drink it. It's good for shock.'

Kelly took a sip and then made a face.

'Go on. Drink up.'

She shook her head. 'Sorry Gran. I can't,' she whispered.

Mum just sat with the cup of tea in front of her on the table, stirring it round and round with a spoon.

Nat scraped back his chair and left the room, and they heard him pounding up the stairs.

The kitchen clock ticked away the minutes. Kelly glanced at it. Only two-thirty.

They heard cars driving up and down the street, the sound of voices, neighbours talking to each other. The world still turning.

Kelly stood up. 'I think I'll ... ' she didn't finish the sentence.

What she meant was that she wanted to be alone. She went into her room and lay on her bed, her hands laced behind her head.

This is it, then. This is the end of it all.

She felt sick. Mum had mentioned the news. Would it be reported – on the telly, in the papers, the radio? She couldn't bear the thought of reporters hanging round again, asking questions, invading their misery. She cried softly into her pillow. Then all this stuff really had been in her imagination. The man she thought was Dad, the mystery about the fight at the pub.

Lizzie had been right all along. Dad was dead. He was never coming back.

But first, she thought of Jack. Jack who had believed it all. Gone along with it. She reached for her phone and texted him.

They've found Dad's ...

She hesitated over the word 'remains', shivering with revulsion as she typed it. But what else could they be, after all this time?

She was about to send it when she remembered what Jack had said. Surely it didn't matter now, did it? Her finger hovered over the 'send' button. Then she deleted the text. He'd find out soon enough anyway.

Ten

Kelly lay on her bed for ages. She knew she would have to accept it now. Mum had said it was 90% certain it was Dad, subject to further forensic tests.

90%. Not completely then?

Stop it! This is the end, Kelly. This really is the end.

She heaved herself up at last, bent down and crawled under the bed to get Dad's picture. Then she walked over to the window and held it up, staring at it.

It was so alive. Such a strong, assured picture. How could he paint that just before he died? Was he already planning to take his life, even then?

What happened, Dad? What was it that was so dreadful you couldn't go on?

She looked at her watch. Lizzie hadn't been in the lesson when Kelly had left; she was in a different set and she'd be coming out of school about now, waiting for Kelly, wondering why she wasn't there. Or perhaps someone had told her she'd gone home. But she wouldn't know why.

As if on cue, her phone rang and Lizzie's name came up.

'Hi babe. They said you'd gone home early. You OK?'

'Not really.' Hearing Lizzie's voice choked her up.

'Kell, you sound dreadful. What's happened?'

Kelly took a deep breath, trying to compose herself. 'The police came round,' she said quietly. 'They've … they've found him.'

There was a shocked silence. Then, 'Your dad?'

'Yeah. Well … what's left of him.'

'Oh Kelly! Listen, I'm on my way round. I'll be with you in half an hour.'

Kelly broke down then. 'Thanks,' she stuttered through her tears.

She stood staring at her phone for a moment, then switched it off. She could hear the sounds of voices downstairs, muffled, talking quietly, and normal things going on, the noise of the dishwasher humming, the fridge door opening and closing. She walked downstairs slowly and joined the rest of the family in the kitchen.

She looked from one face to the other. All showing signs of shock, but there was something else, too. It was as though they'd all been holding their breath for the past four years, never quite accepting what had happened. And now … well now they could let that breath go.

Dad was dead. Dad was really dead. He would never come back. She would never see him again.

Nat was there, looking so young and sad that Kelly's

heart skipped a beat. Gone was the nonchalant, don't care about anything, geeky twelve-year-old. He was just a lad who had loved his father. Had he, too, been holding on to some mad belief that maybe Dad hadn't died?

And Mum; her eyes red from crying and her face so pale.

Only Gran seemed unchanged. She stomped round the kitchen clearing things away and sorting out stuff for their tea as if her life depended on it.

When Lizzie came round, the barriers broke down further and at last they spoke about him – and Nat voiced what they'd all been thinking.

'Well, at least now we know for sure.'

Gran nodded and put her hand on his shoulder. For once he didn't shrug it off.

'I expect there'll be stuff in the papers,' said Mum.

Gran frowned. 'Oh, I dunno. It's old news, isn't it. Probably just a mention. Nothing like when he disappeared.'

'Oh God. I hope not,' muttered Mum. 'I couldn't go through that again. All those horrible journalists … '

Just as Lizzie was about to go, the doorbell rang and they all jumped.

'Oh no!' whispered Mum, peering out of the lounge window at the young man on the doorstep.

Lizzie was beside her. 'It's OK,' she said, 'It's only Jack.'

'Who's Jack?'

Kelly heard. 'Just a friend from school,' she said quickly, going to the door and opening it.

Jack was standing there looking embarrassed. He was holding a bunch of flowers that he'd obviously bought from the garage at the end of the street. He held them out.

'I just wanted to say how sorry … '

Kelly smiled at him and took the flowers. 'You heard, then? Thanks.' And for some reason, seeing him standing there, shifting from one foot to the other, made her want to cry all over again.

'Come in for a minute,' she said.

He looked down at his feet. 'I don't want to … like … intrude.'

'You're not – it's good to see you,' said Kelly.

'You sure?'

She nodded and Jack shambled in.

She introduced him to Mum.

'Thank you for coming,' said Mum, then she showed Lizzie out and went back into the kitchen with Nat and Gran, leaving Kelly and Jack alone together in the lounge.

For a few moments neither of them said anything. Eventually Kelly sighed and said, 'I suppose this is it. It's over. I was stupid to think there was any mystery about his death. Obviously he took his own life.'

Jack looked up. 'Don't you want to find out why?'

'What?'

Jack blushed. 'Sorry, that was crass. I just wondered if it might help to go on … '

'You mean go on digging?'

'Only if you want to, Kelly.'

'Oh, I dunno Jack. It won't make any difference, will it? Not now.'

'Well … '

She frowned. 'Well what? You haven't found out something have you?'

Jack sat down heavily in a chair. 'Not me,' he said, 'But it was something my dad let slip when I was talking to him about ... about the case. Something that got me thinking.'

'What?'

She really wasn't sure she wanted to know now, but Jack seemed eager to get it off his chest.

'You know my dad said they came up against a blank wall whenever they tried to find out stuff about your dad's background. You know, there was a sort of gap between uni and when he went to art college, when he seemed to just drift?'

She sighed. 'Yeah. You said. And Mum said he never really found out what he wanted to do until he went to art college.'

'Well. What if he was doing something dodgy all that time?'

Kelly had been curled in a chair, her eyes half closed, but at this she sat up straight and stared at Jack.

'Stop it,' she said angrily. 'You didn't know him, Jack. He was the straightest guy in the world. He just ... well he wouldn't be capable of doing anything dodgy.'

Jack bit his lip. 'Keep your hair on Kelly. It ... it was just an idea.'

Suddenly Kelly had had enough. She jumped up out of her chair.

'Shut up, Jack. I'm not listening to any more of this. Just leave me alone. I want to be with my family.'

She ran down the passage and into the kitchen, straight into Mum's arms, trembling with rage. How *dare* Jack say that!

'Kelly ... love.' Mum hugged her tight and stroked her hair.

After a moment, they heard footsteps in the hall and the front door being quietly shut.

Kelly disentangled herself from Mum's embrace.

'I can't face seeing anyone,' she said. 'Not just yet.'

Gran came over and took Kelly's hand. 'It won't be like the first time,' she said. 'There won't be a lot of interest. I promise you.'

'How do you know? They could start digging up everything all over again.'

Gran shook her head. 'No. As I said, it's old news.'

It turned out that Gran was right. There was a small piece on the local telly news and a paragraph in the local paper, but that was it. No hordes of reporters in the street. No real interest at all.

'Case resolved. Man's remains found.'

For the next couple of days, Kelly and Nat stayed off school and Mum and Gran were at home, too, in case Dad's death sparked any renewed interest in the Press, but there was nothing, and both Kelly and Nat went back to school.

On the first day back, Lizzie came round to fetch Kelly and they walked down the street together.

'How are you?'

Kelly shrugged. 'It's better at home. At least we're talking about him now. Now that it's definite.'

'And you've … '

Kelly turned to her. 'Accepted it? Yeah. I haven't got a choice, have I?'

'Good. So, you'll all be able to move on.'

'God, Lizzie, you sound like that bleeding counsellor! "Move on!" Where to, exactly? It's a stupid phrase.'

'Only trying to help.'

Kelly took Lizzie's arm and squeezed it. 'I know. I'm just a grumpy cow. Let's drop it. Tell me about the play. Are Mark and the witch back together again?'

'No way. Talk about chilly. You should see how they freeze each other out. So, Kelly Wilson, now's your chance.'

But somehow, Kelly couldn't raise any enthusiasm.

I can't believe it. Now I'll get the chance to see him while I'm working on the scenery and I just can't be bothered. What's wrong with me?

During the next few days Kelly found it difficult to focus on school work, and the only time she was absorbed when she was working on the scenery for the play.

They were in the theatre now, so they could see everything in place, and the date for the production was getting closer.

Kelly helped to design the poster, too. 'Christmas Production of Romeo and Juliet,' it shrieked. And there was a wonderful shot of Lizzie and Mark in costume, looking into each other's eyes.

Christmas meant the visit to see Uncle John. Kelly shut her mind to it and concentrated on doing the best job she could on the scenery.

She and her art teacher went to one of the rehearsals, to see how the producer and the cast reacted to it. They were full of praise.

'Hey, it's amazing. Don't know how you've made it so real.'

'That wall looks so solid – and all the plants. You want to reach out and touch them.'

Kelly and her teacher sat right at the back of the theatre to gauge the effect.

'It's brilliant,' said her teacher. 'Even better than I'd hoped.'

Kelly grinned. Her teacher left after a while, but Kelly stayed on to watch the rehearsal.

Although Shakespeare wasn't really her thing, she found herself becoming completely bound up in the story – and when Mark and Lizzie were on stage, there was no doubting the chemistry between them.

The door at the back of the theatre opened and someone came in and sat beside Kelly. It was dark and she was too wrapped up in the play to notice who it was, but when there was a break for some technical hitch and the lights went on again, she saw it was Jack.

'Hi,' he said.

'Hi.' She felt embarrassed. He'd been kind to come and see her and bring her flowers and everything, and she'd bitten his head off.

'You OK?' he asked.

She nodded. 'Sort of.'

They talked about the play then. Neutral ground.

'I came to see how Mark is shaping up as Romeo,' said Jack.

'Pretty well, I'd say. And Lizzie's brilliant as Juliet. I know they're only acting, but the love thing's pretty convincing.'

'Very!' said Jack, laughing. 'You'd almost think … '

'What! You don't … ?'

'*You'd* know if they were,' said Jack. 'You're that thick with Lizzie.'

'I don't think so,' said Kelly slowly.

But maybe they are falling for one another. Maybe Lizzie's in denial. Oh, what do I know? One thing's for sure, he's never going to look that way at me.

Jack had said something, but she hadn't heard.

'Sorry?'

'D'you fancy grabbing a quick drink after this?'

'I said I'd go home with Lizzie.'

'Oh. OK.'

She smiled at him then. 'Maybe another time – and Jack, I'm sorry I yelled at you when you came round. I was just feeling … so rubbish.'

'Sure,' said Jack.

Jack left shortly after that and Kelly waited for Lizzie. As they were walking home, Kelly took her arm.

'You and Mark – you're really good. Brilliant casting.'

Lizzie made a face. 'I'm enjoying it. He's good to act with.'

'Hmm. Just acting is it?'

'Duh! Of course it is! How many times!' But Kelly noticed that she was blushing. Lizzie changed the subject. 'Dress rehearsal next week. It's getting that close. I can't believe it.'

They talked for a while about what Lizzie would be wearing, and when they parted, Lizzie said. 'You OK, babe?'

'Yeah. I'm OK.'

Kelly's phone vibrated just as she was reaching her door. A text from Jack. Now that Dad's 'remains' had been found, Jack obviously thought they could stop the cloak and dagger stuff.

Good to see you. Coffee on Sun?
Same time/place?

Kelly hesitated before replying. She wasn't sure she wanted to get too close to Jack, but she liked him – and he was the only person who'd believed her about Dad. Maybe she owed him.

She texted back.

OK see you then.

She made a bit more effort this time, washing her unruly hair and putting on a new top. Jack wasn't there when she arrived at the coffee shop, but she saw him in the distance, crossing the road, hurrying towards her, taking great strides with his long legs, a huge grin on his face.

They sat down and ordered their drinks.

'You been OK?' he asked.

She looked down at the table surface. 'It's been hard … '

'Yeah. When you thought all along there might be a chance … '

She nodded.

Jack leant forward and for a moment she thought he was going to take her hand, but instead he whispered.

'I was at the pub last night.'

Kelly frowned.

Why the hell is he telling me about his under-age drinking, though he could get away with it, I suppose. He looks at least eighteen.

'You know. *The* pub.'

She still looked puzzled.

'The pub where your dad had the fight.'

Kelly jerked her head up and met his eyes. 'What?'

'Yeah. It was bizarre. I was biking down the canal path. I don't often go home that way, there's too many people around, you can't get up any speed.'

Kelly's stare was still hostile and he dropped his eyes. 'Anyway, I saw the pub sign.'

Kelly started to stand up. She felt really angry with him.

'For god's sake Jack! Stop it! It's all over. There's no point.'

He reached out and held onto her arm to stop her leaving.

'But it's not, Kelly,' he said very quietly. 'I don't think it *is* all over.'

She stared at him, furious. 'And I don't want to hear any more.'

'Don't go, Kelly,' he said. 'Let me just explain.'

She shook off his arm. 'You're upsetting me, Jack. Stop it.' But she sank back into her chair, her hands over her eyes.

She couldn't concentrate on what he was saying.

Dad's gone. He's dead. He's never coming back.

'Did you hear what I said?'

She shook her head

'I was just going to check outside, have a look at the place – but I was well thirsty and I fancied a Coke.'

She looked at him. 'So?' she said wearily.

'Well, it was full, being a Saturday night, and I found

myself standing next to this boring guy who was obviously looking for someone to talk to.'

Kelly said nothing, so he continued. 'He was going on about how he'd lived round the area for years and this was his local. I wasn't really listening, but then I suddenly thought that if he was a regular, he might have known your dad.'

'Oh for goodness sake, Jack. I really don't want to know.'

He ignored her. 'He didn't know him – but he *did* remember the fight!'

She felt a tiny prickle of interest. 'Did he say anything about the other guy?'

'He didn't get the chance. Suddenly someone knocked into him and spilt his beer all over his clothes. He was really pissed off and made this big fuss.'

'So … '

'I swear it wasn't an accident.'

'For heaven's sake. You said the place was crowded.'

'Yeah. But … '

'But what?'

'When I left the pub I couldn't find my phone.'

Kelly frowned.

'I *knew* it had been in my pocket. There was no way it had fallen out. So I went back into the pub and it was on the bar. The landlord said someone had just found it and handed it to him.'

She shrugged. 'It happens.'

'No, it doesn't. Not like that. It was safe in my pocket. I know it was. Someone took it while the guy was fussing about his beer, people were trying to help him, everyone was looking at him.'

'So, you're saying someone stole it – and then had a fit of conscience and handed it in? That's ridiculous.'

'Yes.'

Kelly took a swig of his coffee. 'Now you're being paranoid.'

'Am I? Think about it, Kell. Someone had my phone for fifteen minutes. That would give them plenty of time.'

They both knew what he meant.

'But why?' said Kelly. 'Why should anyone want to … you know … keep tabs on you.'

'The only reason I can think of is because of my … because of you and me.'

'There is no "you and me",' she said sharply.

He blushed. 'I mean that we're friends.'

There was an awkward silence.

She shifted in her chair and sighed. 'You're still going on about Dad?'

He nodded. 'It's the only reason I can think of.'

'Dad's dead,' she said flatly.

Jack looked out of the window. 'Maybe someone out there still doesn't believe he's dead,' he said softly.

'Oh for god's sake, this is doing my head in,' she whispered. 'The police found his remains. What more proof does anyone need?'

'But if he *is* dead,' said Jack, still speaking very softly. 'Don't you still want to know what happened? Don't you want to know *why* he took his own life?'

She scraped back her chair and grabbed her bag. 'Leave it!' she hissed and then, without looking back, she ran out onto the pavement.

Eleven

All the way home on the bus, thoughts were whirling around in Kelly's head.

Damn him! Damn him for stirring it up again.

The questions came back. What was Dad doing before he met Mum? Why had Gran cut those pages from her diary? What were Gran and Mum talking about when she'd overheard that conversation? Who was the man at the pub?

And the business about Jack's phone. Was Jack just being paranoid? Who knew he'd gone to the pub? Had he been followed there. Was someone following her too?

Dad's dead. Stop this! No one's following anyone.

As she walked up her street, someone called to her and she spun round.

'Hey,' said Lizzie, coming up to her. 'It's only me!'

'Sorry, I was miles away.'

Lizzie took her arm. 'I was just coming over. Your phone's off.'

Kelly took it out of her pocket. After leaving the café she'd not felt like talking to anyone.

'Oh yeah. Sorry.'

Lizzie stopped and held her at arms length. 'You look good, Kelly Wilson. Have you been on a date?'

There was no deceiving her. Kelly sighed. 'Sort of.'

'Sort of?'

'I just met Jack for coffee in town,' she mumbled.

'Hmm,' said Lizzie. 'For someone who absolutely does not fancy that boy, you're seeing a lot of him.'

'Well ... '

'Well what?'

'Well, I do *like* him.'

Why did I say that. I am furious with him.

'Ha!'

Maybe it's best to pretend.

'He's growing on me.'

'Hey, is this a budding romance?'

Kelly shook her head. 'Nah, but he's ... well he's really easy to talk to.'

'You keep saying that. So what exactly do you talk about?'

'Oh, I dunno. He thinks you and Mark are falling for each other.'

There, Lizzie. Turning the tables on you, girl!

'We are NOT,' laughed Lizzie.

'Hmm,' said Kelly. 'Then why are you blushing?'

'OK, OK, subject closed. Let's talk about your birthday.'

'My birthday?'

'Don't tell me you've forgotten you're going to be fifteen next week?'

Kelly smiled. 'You know, with everything else going on … and no one's mentioned it at home. Maybe they've forgotten, too.'

'No they haven't. Your mum's been onto me about arranging something.'

'Mum. Really? She's been so … '

'Distracted?'

'Yeah. She's been all over the place since the police … '

'I know,' said Lizzie quietly. 'But she still wants to do something special for you, and she was looking for ideas.'

'I don't want any fuss.'

'Well, OK. But you need to go out somewhere. How about bowling or skating – or hot air ballooning?'

'*What?*'

'Well, maybe not hot air ballooning. Oh, you know, Kell, something fun and silly, take you out of yourself.'

Kelly smiled. 'Yeah. That would be good. But … well I know it's mad but, I'd sort of like Nat to be in on it, too. It's been really hard on him, you know, all this about Dad.'

'OK, so what does he like?'

Kelly laughed. 'Chess!'

'Yeah. Like that's going to happen!'

Kelly shrugged. 'And his bike.'

Lizzie's eyebrows shot up. 'That's a big ask!'

'Forget it. I'm happy with vegging out with some soppy film.'

'No way,' said Lizzie slowly. 'I'll have a think – and talk to your mum.'

'OK. Whatever.'

'And,' continued Lizzie. 'How do you feel about asking Jack … and maybe Mark, too?'

Kelly smiled. '"And maybe Mark, too?"' she repeated.

Lizzie blushed again. 'Well, if you're going to have Nat, it would be company for him wouldn't it, to have a couple of blokes along?'

'Umm. Maybe, I dunno.'

'Leave it with me. I need to see your mum.'

In the house, Lizzie disappeared into the kitchen with Kelly's mum, and Kelly could hear a lot of whispering and laughter going on. When they emerged, they were both smiling.

'Lizzie's had the most brilliant idea for your birthday,' said Mum.

'Oh yeah, what's that?'

'Oh no,' said Lizzie. 'I'm not telling. Not until it's fixed. It may not … well it may not work, so I can't tell you yet. I'm off home to do some serious online research.'

'Have a sandwich before you go,' said Mum.

'No, I'll grab something at home. I won't have much time. I've got another rehearsal this afternoon.'

When Lizzie had left, Kelly frowned. 'This all sounds a bit sinister,' she said.

Mum gave her a hug. 'No, it's a great idea if we can sort it,' she said. 'Just what we all need.'

She looks happier. Not so tense. Maybe hearing about Dad was a good thing.

Kelly went up to her room. She'd said she was going to do some homework, but she couldn't concentrate. In the end she gave up. Once more, she dragged Dad's picture out from under her bed. She knew she'd have to take it back up to the attic before someone noticed it had gone, but she wanted a last look at it.

Somehow, it seemed even more significant now. She peered between the figures of the man and the girl sitting under the tree and then back to the distant, vague figure at the edge of the trees, half obscured.

It's him! He's painted himself with me, and then without me, going away. Is that why he came back to the park, because it meant so much to him?

He didn't come back. He's dead.

Mum was out and Gran was busy cooking, so Kelly picked up the picture and tiptoed across the landing. She let down the attic ladder as quietly as she could and climbed up.

In the attic, she put the picture back and then started looking at the paintings left there. Would Mum sell some of them now?

She crouched down, going through them carefully, sometimes taking one out to look at it.

'What are you doing?'

She hadn't heard him. She'd been so absorbed in what she was doing. She whipped round, still clutching one of the paintings.

Nat had come up the ladder and his head was poking over the top into the attic space. He was frowning.

'I saw the ladder was down,' he said defensively.

Kelly's heartbeat slowed. She smiled at him.

'I was just looking at Dad's work,' she said simply. 'Here, come and join me.'

He hesitated, his dark head framed in the opening, and Kelly could sense his reluctance. Then he slowly climbed up the final steps of the ladder, crawled into the attic and turned to pull the ladder up behind him.

They sat side-by-side, passing the paintings between each other. Kelly didn't think that Nat had been interested in Dad's work, but she could see him looking closely at them, taking his time.

'I don't know anything about art,' he mumbled. 'But I guess he was quite good, wasn't he? He must have been if people bought his pictures.'

She nodded. 'The best.'

'Will … will Mum keep all these?'

Kelly shrugged. 'I don't know,' she said slowly. 'I think Dad would rather people bought them and looked at them.'

'Better than being hidden up here?'

'Umm.'

She took a deep breath. 'I guess she was hanging onto them until … well, until it was definite that he'd died.'

Nat was silent and Kelly realised he was struggling to hold back tears. She looked away.

'Do you remember him, Nat?'

She'd expected him to snap at her, but instead he said, 'Yeah, I remember lots about him, 'specially him teaching me chess and playing with me. And going on bike rides and that. But … '

He sniffed and shifted his position. 'I wish I could remember more,' he said.

'I know,' said Kelly. 'It's four years. There's lots I can't remember.' She bit her lip. 'I hate that I can't … ' She couldn't finish the sentence.

I can't really remember his voice – or his laugh. I hate that he's fading away like this.

'Mum's still got those video clips,' said Nat.

Kelly looked up sharply. No one else had mentioned them. In these past years, she'd not once seen them. Videos taken on holiday, with Dad playing the fool, joking and laughing. And earlier, when Kelly and Nat were much younger, Dad there in the background, his presence always so vivid.

Was he really just acting? Was it all a pretense, a ghastly show? Surely not. Surely he was happy with us?

'Maybe we could look at the videos again,' said Nat. 'You know. To remember … remember what he looked like.'

Kelly nodded. 'Maybe.'

'Now we know he's not coming back.'

Kelly turned to him. He looked so sad.

She put her arm round his shoulders and pulled him towards her and, to her astonishment, he didn't resist and she could feel him sobbing against her. She said nothing and at last he pulled away, rubbing his eyes. Embarrassed, he started to scrabble to his feet and move away from her, but Kelly held onto his arm.

'Nat. We'll always have each other,' she said. 'Even though you are a massive pain in the butt.'

The tension broke and he grinned. 'Not such a massive one as you, Kelly Wilson.'

She let him go then. 'Hey, you know it's my birthday next week?'

''Course.'

'Liar!'

'Well, I do now.'

She smiled. 'I think Mum and Lizzie are planning something special.'

'Oh yeah?'

'And it involves you.'

'Me! No thanks, Kell. Count me out. I don't want to come on some girly outing.'

She shook her head. 'It won't be a girly outing. Not if Lizzie's plans work out.'

'Well, whatever they are, I'm not coming. I expect it's on a chess club night.'

'No it's not,' said Kelly, triumphantly. 'My birthday's on a Wednesday and there's no chess club – or drama club.'

Nat frowned. 'Drama club?'

'Yep. Lizzie's rehearsing for a play and so is ... well never mind. The point is, it is a free night and so there's no excuse.'

'No way!' said Nat, firmly.

'We'll see.'

As they were climbing down the ladder, Gran was coming upstairs.

'What are you two doing up there?'

'Looking at Dad's pictures,' said Nat.

Just for a moment, Gran's face registered something. What was it? Shock? Fear? But in seconds, Gran had wiped the expression.

'Your mum needs to decide about those,' she said gruffly.

'Umm,' said Kelly. 'They shouldn't stay up there. They're too good.'

As she went back to her room to have another shot at her homework, she thought about what Nat had said. Those videos of Dad. She'd forgotten all about them. But there was a time when Mum was always filming the three of them on her phone or tablet, and they must be stored somewhere. She wondered if Mum ever looked at the images, reminded herself of what life had been like before he went.

If I get a chance I'll look on Mum's laptop.

The chance came sooner than she'd expected. Mum took Nat off to chess club and said she'd meet up with a friend until he'd finished, and Gran went to see someone who lived the other side of town.

'You be OK on your own, love?' asked Mum.

'*Mum!*'

Mum grinned. 'Oh yes, I'd forgotten. You're almost fifteen!'

'Duh. You're so funny!'

Kelly waved them off, noticing that Mum was only carrying a small bag. Usually, she went everywhere with a big shoulder bag which had a special compartment for her laptop.

Kelly waited until she heard the car reverse out of the garage, then she went into Mum's office. The laptop was on her desk. She hesitated for a moment and then she opened it and started to go through all the folders. Mum was very organised and they were all labelled. And there was the one she was looking for, called 'Family pix'. Kelly swallowed, not sure if she really wanted to look through them. She was used to seeing Dad's face staring out from the few framed photos on the table in the lounge, but this would be different. Most of these were videos: living, moving, speaking images of him.

She sat back and clicked onto the earliest one. Nat as a baby in Dad's arms, with Kelly beside him, a curly-headed three-year-old looking up at him and scowling.

I was dead jealous!

She clicked on through. Happy family videos. No sense of what was to come. Dad looking relaxed, funny, doing stupid things in front of the camera to make them laugh.

She didn't try to hold back the tears as she watched. So many memories. And she didn't notice how much time had gone by until she realised that the sun was going down and the room was getting dark. The others would be back soon. Quickly she clicked through to the last of the videos. The date on it was only a few days before he'd disappeared. On Nat's birthday.

Dad wasn't smiling much in this one. He looked distracted, seemed to be focusing on something in the middle distance. Kelly zoomed in and slowed down the action. She saw that his hands were restless, moving all the time as if he was trying to crush something between them. The camera played on his face for a moment before he turned away, obviously irritated. She replayed it and saw that there was, unmistakably, a fading bruise around his eye. She froze the image and stared at it.

After that fight. Everything had changed after that fight at the pub.

She suddenly heard a noise outside and the sound of the key turning in the front door. Gran was back.

Quickly, Kelly closed the laptop and legged it back to her room. She sat on the edge of her bed, dried her eyes and blew her nose.

Jack's right. I do need to know. Dad may be dead, but I want to know why he died. Why he took his life.

In the press reports, it had said that he was depressed,

but was that true? He looked happy, right up until the time of the incident in the pub. Happy and funny and relaxed. The dad she'd always known.

What had happened to change everything? Who was the guy at the pub? And why had records of the fight been wiped?

It wouldn't leave her alone.

Twelve

Jack was the only person she could confide in, but she'd blown that, hadn't she? Told him to leave it, told him there was no 'You and me'.

He'd only been trying to help and she'd as good as slapped him in the face. She wondered if Lizzie had asked him to come to the birthday surprise she was planning for Kelly. She wouldn't blame him if he'd said no.

He didn't phone. He didn't approach her at school.

On Friday, she saw him in the distance. He was talking to a girl, someone in his year, and unexpectedly Kelly felt a pang of jealousy. She forced it down, knowing she had no right. Before she could think too much about what she was doing, she ran over to them.

'Sorry,' she said as she approached them, conscious that her face was red and her hair wild. 'Can I talk to you, Jack?'

The older girl raised an eyebrow. 'Be my guest,' she said, turning away.

Jack looked after her.

'Sorry,' said Kelly again.

Jack sighed. 'What do you want, Kelly?'

He wasn't smiling and suddenly she felt really stupid.

She looked down at her feet. 'I've missed you,' she mumbled.

Why did I say that? But it's true, I have missed him.

There was a long silence and Kelly felt her face burning up.

Jack folded his arms and looked down at her. 'Say that again.'

She thought she might cry with embarrassment.

'I've missed you,' she repeated.

He gave a faint smile and she felt her heart skip a beat.

'You were right,' she went on, so quietly that he had to lean down to hear her.

'Right about what?'

'I do want to know more. I want to know why Dad did it. And what happened at that pub.'

There was another awkward silence. Kelly could feel Jack's eyes on her.

'Is that the only reason you want to see me, Kelly?' he said at last. 'Just because you think I can help you find out stuff?'

She shook her head and put her hand out shyly to touch his arm. He didn't move away and she left it there. Then, slowly, he covered her hand with his, curling his fingers under her palm.

The bell went.

Jack gently removed her hand. He cleared his throat. 'OK. Meet me at Millennium Park tomorrow afternoon.'

'What! That's miles away.'

'And come on your bike! You need the practice.'

'What are you on about?'

'Your birthday.'

So he is coming! And Lizzie's been onto him already. She's planning something involving bikes for my birthday, so that Nat and Jack and Mark can join in. That is such a bad idea. There's nothing good about being seen on a bike, all sweaty and red in the face. What's she even thinking about?

Everyone was streaming back into class.

'See you there at half-past two tomorrow.' Jack turned away before she could answer, but she smiled, still feeling the warmth of his hand on hers.

The next morning, she dragged her bike out of the shed in the back garden. She couldn't even remember when she'd last ridden it. It was dusty and covered in cobwebs and the tyres looks suspiciously spongy.

I can't ride this! I'll take the bus.

A window opened and Nat leaned out. 'You're not going for a *ride*, Kell?'

She looked up. 'Nah. It was just an idea, but my bike's a real mess.'

'I'll come and take a look,' said Nat, closing the window. The next moment he was out in the garden, pulling on his hoodie against the cold, damp December air. He took the bike from her.

'Just needs a wipe down and the tyres pumped up,' he said.

'It's probably got a puncture,' she said hopefully.

I don't want him to sort it. I really don't want to ride it.

But Nat was already on the job. He'd found the pump and was inflating the tyres until they were firm, then he took a rag and got rid of the worst of the spiders' webs and dust.

'Go on. Give it a go.'

God. I suppose I'll have to, now he's gone to all that trouble.

She wheeled the bike down the path to the front gate and out onto the street. Nat followed her and watched as she gingerly mounted then rode off down the road, wobbling as she adjusted to being on board.

Nat cupped his hands over his mouth and yelled after her. 'You're doing great,' he said.

Kelly muttered to herself. She rode down to Lizzie's house, wheeled the bike up the path and banged on the door. When Lizzie saw her she burst out laughing.

'What?'

'You look so cross!'

'I'm cross with you. I know what you're planning.'

Lizzie grinned. 'I have no idea what you mean,' she said. 'I've just done what you asked and found something that Nat will enjoy – and Jack and Mark.'

'You've already asked Jack, haven't you?'

'Might have.'

'I *know* you have.'

Lizzie raised an eyebrow. 'You're very thick, you two,' she said.

Kelly looked down at the ground. Lizzie went on. 'Jack didn't tell you, did he?'

'Tell me what?'

'What we're going to do on Wednesday?'

Kelly shook her head. 'Just that it apparently involves bikes – and because of that, Lizzie Stewart, I may have to kill you. Biking anywhere involves going red in the face and getting sweaty – and in December, for goodness sake. Biking somewhere in December! I can't believe you!'

'You'll love it,' said Lizzie, grinning. 'And your mum's really excited about it.'

'Mum's excited – about biking? *That* I cannot believe.'

'I'm absolutely saying nothing more,' said Lizzie. 'Now off you go, do some practising. I've got a rehearsal.'

'Oh yeah. The dress rehearsal. Good luck with that.'

'Thanks. First performance Friday night, then two performances on the Saturday. Have you got your tickets?'

''Course.'

'I really have to go,' said Lizzie. 'Happy biking,' she said, as she closed the door.

'Huh!'

Kelly rode on down the street and round the corner. She was beginning to feel a bit more confident, but already she could feel the strain on little-used muscles. As she rode around the area, despite herself, she started to enjoy it, riding up and down streets which were off her usual routes to the shops and to school. At first she'd been shivering with cold, but the more she cycled, the warmer she became. She experimented with going a bit faster and, as the wind caught her hair, she found she was laughing.

Nat was waiting for her as she sailed back up their street and braked at their gate.

'Looking good,' he said, rubbing his hands together and blowing on them.

'You're a rubbish liar, Nat Wilson,' said Kelly as she dismounted.

'No, honest. You look good on a bike!'

She gave him a death stare and he started to giggle.

It's such a long time since I've seen him smiling, let alone really laughing.

'Anyway,' said Nat. 'Why are you suddenly interested in your bike?'

Ah. Obviously no one's told him.

'I'm going to meet a friend this afternoon,' she said. 'He's a keen biker and we're going to meet up in the Millennium Park.'

Nat's eyes widened. 'Is he a boyfriend, Kell?'

'Nah. He's just a mate.'

'Oh. OK. Look, I'll clean it up properly for you. Make it look good.'

He inspected the tyres. 'They're still hard, there's no slow puncture or anything, Kell.'

'Pity,' she mumbled.

He looked up, frowning. 'Don't you want me to … ?'

Don't be an ungrateful pig.

'If you've got time, that would be great. Thanks, Nat.'

As she turned to go in the house, she heard him whistling tunelessly as he carefully polished and wiped.

She'd *have* to go now.

She set off in the afternoon. Millennium Park was the other side of the town and she had no idea how long it would take her to get there, so she allowed plenty of time – time for being held up in traffic and getting lost – but the Sunday streets were pretty empty and she made no mistakes in the route, so she got to the park early. There was no sign of Jack, so she wheeled her bike over to a bench and sat down.

Why did he ask me to meet him here, for god's sake? Another park. Another reminder of Dad.

It was a cold, dreary overcast day, not the sort of day to tempt you outside, but she spotted some families over in the big play area and heard shrieks of laughter from the children as they were pushed on the swings or slid down the slide or bounced up and down on the other equipment.

She'd been really warm when she arrived, after all the exertion, but after a while she started to shiver. She zipped up her jacket and put her hands in her pockets, then started pacing up and down. It was well past two-thirty.

Come on Jack. You're late.

She tried phoning him, but his phone was switched off.

When her teeth started to chatter, she got on her bike and started to ride slowly round the perimeter of the park, gradually warming up again. She'd already done a full circuit and had almost given up on Jack.

He's not coming. This is all a sick joke. He's paying me back for shouting at him. He doesn't even fancy me. He fancies that girl he was talking to at break. God, I'm such an idiot.

Then she heard someone shout her name. She looked up and saw a lycra-clad, helmeted figure hurtling towards her on what looked like a racing bike, a large backpack slung over his shoulders. Even with all the biking gear on, there was no mistaking those long gangly legs. Jack slowed down as he approached and slithered to a stop beside her.

'Sorry,' he puffed. 'Took longer … than I … thought.'

'I … I thought you weren't coming,' she said. I thought …'

Jack removed his helmet and put his hand through his hair. 'I'm really sorry. They kept us late at the club'

Kelly was close to tears.

What is wrong with me?

She swallowed and sniffed. 'Why did you want us to meet here, for goodness sake? It's miles from my house.'

Jack smiled. 'Yeah. But close to the cycling club! And you need to practice.'

Jack leant his bike against the nearest bench and then slipped off his backpack. Kelly followed him, still scowling, her head a jumble of confused emotions, while he held his side and took some deep breaths. 'Just give me a minute. I broke every speed limit getting here.'

Kelly sighed and folded her arms.

At last he turned and looked at her. Then he smiled and she couldn't help herself; she smiled back. He stretched out his hand and pulled her towards him.

God, I really want him to kiss me.

But he didn't kiss her. He just held her close for a few moments and then released her, before sitting down on the bench. Kelly sat down close to him.

'Sure you want to go on with this?' asked Jack.

It took her a moment to realise he was talking about her dad.

She looked across at the ever-moving, darting scene of the little children away over in the play area.

Do I?

She looked down and put her hands between her knees. 'What do you think?'

He was quiet for so long that she repeated the question.

'I had a long talk with my dad last night,' he said. 'And … and I came clean about why I was really looking into your dad's death.'

Kelly's head snapped up. 'You *what*? What were you thinking … ?'

'Hear me out, Kell. If your dad was doing something dodgy – and yes, I know it's a big if – but *if* he was, then he may have taken his life to protect you.'

Kelly stared at him. 'What?'

Jack went on. 'Anyway, my dad said we should keep well out of it. That poking around isn't going to achieve anything … and that it could get us into trouble.'

'So, you're going to leave it, then?'

Jack stood up and started to put on his helmet. 'It's your call, Kelly.'

Kelly struggled to her feet, stiff with the cold now. She dragged a tissue from her pocket and blew her nose.

'I just want to know,' she whispered. Then she cleared her throat. 'I just want to know the truth.'

'Even though he can't come back to you?'

She nodded.

'But you know we may never find out?'

'Yeah. I know,' she said quietly.

'And that we'll be on our own?'

She nodded.

'OK,' he said slowly. 'Try and think of anyone he might have confided in – a friend or relation. Anyone who was close to him.'

'I don't think Mum or Gran … '

'Anyone else?'

She shook her head. 'I'll try and think.'

'Good. And hey?'

'What?'

'I'm really looking forward to Wednesday.'

'Wednesday?'

'Your birthday!'

She made a face. 'I don't know what Lizzie and Mum have been plotting, but I know I'm going to hate it.'

He grinned. 'You will not. Come on, get on your bike. We'll ride back together.'

Thirteen

For the next couple of days Kelly wandered about in a strange kind of limbo. Lizzie was so wrapped up in last-minute rehearsals she hardly saw her – and Jack was still insisting they didn't phone one another. He was convinced that someone had put a tracking device on his phone, so they only spoke to each other at school, in snatched moments at break times.

She had to put up with a lot of teasing from her friends. 'Thought you had the hots for Mark, Kelly. What's with the Jack thing?'

She went along with it. 'He's nice. I like him.'

'Ooooo! What about Mark, then?'

'What about him?'

'Abandoned hope there?'

She had smiled. 'Yeah. He's well out of my league.'

When she was on her own, she thought a lot about what Jack had said. About whether Dad may have confided in someone.

How much did Mum know?

And Gran? She was sure Gran knew something – otherwise why had she cut those pages from her diary? But surely if she did know anything, she'd have told Mum. Wouldn't she? Maybe she wouldn't. Maybe she was protecting Mum. But what *had* she been saying to Mum when Kelly had overheard them talking that night? Had Gran thought that maybe, after some time, Dad *would* come back? Had she encouraged Mum to think that?

She tried to remember Dad's friends. Everyone had loved him; he must have had some good friends. Who had come round to the house after he'd disappeared?

It was no good. She'd been in such a state herself then that she simply couldn't remember. It was such a long time ago – and she'd only been ten at the time.

But she had to try.

She was still thinking about it when she was helping clear up after tea, and at first she didn't hear what Mum said.

'What do you think, Kell?'

'Sorry. What?'

'I knew you weren't listening. I said, what do you think about selling some of Dad's paintings?'

Kelly looked up, surprised. 'Has Gran been on at you?'

'Yes, she mentioned them. And she's right. But we should choose some to keep, too. To remind us of him.'

She really has accepted it now. That we're not going to see him again.

'Yeah. Do you … do you want me to look through them with you?'

Mum stripped off her rubber gloves and slapped them down on the sink.

'Yes. Why don't we do that right now? Let's go up to the attic and have a sort out.'

It didn't take all that long. Kelly had already decided on the ones she liked best – the ones she felt they should keep – and Mum chose another couple she was fond of.

As they sat on the floor, dividing up the paintings, Kelly sensed that the subject of Dad was no longer off limits. Now that they knew he was dead, the taboo had been lifted.

'How did you and Dad meet?' asked Kelly.

Mum smiled and sat back, leaning against the wall.

'It was so stupid. It was an accident.'

'An accident?'

'Yes, I was getting off a bus and I tripped. I'd been shopping and all my bags flew out of my hands and landed on the pavement. Dad was getting off behind me and he helped me pick them up and – and well, we just clicked and he walked home with me.'

So there were no mutual friends, no history.

'Was he at art college then?'

Mum shook her head. 'No. He enrolled a few months later.'

When he was sure she was the one, perhaps.

Why didn't I know this? Why have I never heard this story before?

As they made their way down from the attic, Mum said, 'Your birthday tomorrow. Are you looking forward to your surprise?'

'I dunno. Not if it involves bikes!'

Mum laughed. 'You'll love it. It was such a brilliant idea of Lizzie's.'

'Umm. She's got a lot to answer for.'

She saw Jack briefly the next day. 'Happy birthday, Kelly. I'll give you your present tonight, at the … '

'The what?'

'Never mind!'

'Oh for goodness sake! And I don't expect a present.'

'Too late,' he said.

She and Lizzie went home from school together. Lizzie ran up the path to her own house.

'See you in a bit. I've just got to change.'

Kelly was hardly inside the door before Mum greeted her. 'Quick, go and change into some jeans. They'll be here any minute.'

Nat was standing behind Mum, grinning fit to burst.

'Happy birthday, Kell,' he said.

She looked at him surprised. 'You're all keen to come now, are you?'

He nodded. 'Now I know where we're going.'

Changing took ages. She simply could not decide which jeans to wear and what top and shoes. She was still dithering when she heard a car draw up outside. She peered out of her bedroom window.

The car seemed to be covered with bikes – a couple on the top and another on a rack at the back. She frowned. Then she saw Jack and Mark climb out of the car, followed by Mark's dad. The next moment they were at the door and she heard the sound of laughter as Mum let them in.

She'd been expecting Mark – but Mark's dad? His dad, who'd been at college with Mum?

Shut up, Kelly. I don't suppose he really fancies her. It was all in your imagination.

Oh god! What if she fancies him? What if … oh for heaven's sake. Of course he had to come. We couldn't all have gone in the one car.

She felt flustered as she ran down the stairs and even more flustered when Mark and Jack handed her a package. 'It's from us both,' said Jack.

'Bring it with you,' said Mum. 'Open it later.'

Gran hustled them out of the door and waved as there was a rush to get into the cars and a bit of jostling to see who was going to go with whom. In the end, Jack, Nat and Kelly went with Mum, and Lizzie went with Mark and his dad.

Kelly sat in front with Mum, and she was surprised when Mum headed onto the motorway and drove south.

'Where are we going?'

'You'll see!'

'Are we going to London?'

'Sort of.'

Nat giggled.

'What?'

'Nothing.'

After nearly an hour, Jack suddenly said. 'Here. It's here.' He was pointing out of the window to something up ahead and Kelly turned back to follow his finger.

'Is that … ?'

'Yay,' shrieked Nat. 'It's the Olympic Park.'

'Don't tell me we're going to ride bikes there?'

'Yep,' said Jack. 'Your mum's booked us a session at the velodrome.'

'And then a meal at the café,' said Mum.

'But I haven't got a bike,' said Kelly.

Jack was leaning forward. 'They'll hire you one – and Lizzie, too. It's all sorted.'

'But I'm rubbish at riding a bike,' wailed Kelly.

'Don't worry,' said Mum. 'You and Lizzie will be going on a beginner's session, then the boys will go on a more advanced one.'

'MUM!'

But, despite herself, Kelly began to feel quite excited as they approached the velodrome and parked the cars. The older boys took the bikes off Mark's dad's car and wheeled them towards the entrance, Nat running along beside them. She had to smile. She'd never seen Nat so excited about anything. Mark had lent him his second racing bike and it was much better than Nat's. He'd adjusted it so it was right for his height, too.

She'd seen pictures of the velodrome on telly, but inside it was really impressive with its curved wooden race track and the high roof making everything echoey.

'OK, girls,' said Mum. 'Your session's about to start. Off you go.'

Lizzie and Kelly made their way down to the group of instructors and other people waiting to join the session. There was a lot of giggling as they were mounted on bikes and given helmets, and a lot of wobbling as they started off round the track, but most of the others were wobbling, too, so they didn't feel too stupid and, as she got more confident, Kelly really started to enjoy herself and tried to remember what she'd been told. By the time their session was over, she was exhausted, but her eyes were shining. She ran back to the others.

'Hey, I actually rode where the Olympic cyclists rode. How cool is that!'

Nat's group was next. He was with other boys of his age and Kelly noticed that he was one of the better riders. Mark and Jack clapped him loudly and he, too, left the track flushed with triumph.

The other two were in an advanced group and they were dead competitive. As they flew round the track, they were vying with each other, and with the others, to get ahead.

Mum was sitting beside Mark's dad. 'Those two are really keen,' she said.

'Yes, they've always been into bikes,' he said. 'Both of them, ever since they were at primary school.'

Later, when they were having a meal in the velodrome café, Kelly opened her presents. A pair of expensive boots from Mum and Gran, a top from Lizzie and a new back light for her bike from Nat. She kept Mark and Jack's present until last.

As she unwrapped it, she started laughing. She held it up.

'A cycle helmet! Are you trying to tell me something?'
Jack grinned.

It was a relaxed meal and there was a lot of laughter. Kelly's mum and Mark's dad were sitting close together and Kelly kept looking at them, trying to see if they were specially friendly, but they gave nothing away.

Just before it was time to leave, Jack got up to go to the toilet.

Kelly watched him as he returned, picking his way through the tables towards them. He was stumbling, knocking into chairs, not looking where he was going, and a couple of times she saw him glance back over his shoulder. He didn't smile when he sat down beside her and she could sense his tension.

'You OK?' whispered Kelly.

He didn't answer.

She frowned, but she didn't have a chance to say anything then because everyone was collecting their things, getting ready to leave. It wasn't until they were standing a bit apart from the others, waiting for Mark's dad to load the bikes, that they had a chance to speak.

'What is it?' said Kelly. 'You looked awful when you came back from the toilet. Are you feeling sick or something?'

Jack swallowed and he looked behind him.

'We've been followed.'

'Followed! Who by? What are you talking about?'

'The bloke from the pub. The one who spilt the guy's drink.'

'*What!* Are you sure?'

He nodded. 'It was definitely him, Kell. He was sitting in the café. At the far side, well away from us. If I'd not gone to the toilet I wouldn't have noticed him.'

Kelly moved closer to Jack. 'Did he ... did he see you?'

'Not then. At least I don't think so. But he knew we were there.' Jack cleared his throat. 'He must have followed us all the way up the motorway.'

'Maybe he was visiting … '

Jack cut her off. 'Just *happening* to visit the velodrome when we're here? You don't believe that, do you? No, he's stalking me, Kelly. He knows where I live, he'll find out who my dad is. And now he knows I know you.'

'But … ' Kelly began.

'It's about your dad, Kell. It *must* be. He thinks I know something.'

His voice had an edge of panic and Kelly reached for his hand. 'I'm sorry. It's all my fault.'

He shook his head. 'No. I was the one who went into that pub and started asking questions.'

'What shall we do?'

'Nothing. What can we do?'

They stood there, in the dark, watching the others fuss round with the bikes.

'I'm scared,' said Kelly. 'What d'you think he wants?'

Jack squeezed her hand. 'I dunno. But I've got a bad feeling about him.'

Jack and Kelly got in the back seat on the way home. They didn't say much, but Nat was banging on about the different bikes he'd seen and how cool it had been, so Mum didn't seem to notice. At one point, she glanced back. 'Did you both enjoy that?'

Jack roused himself. 'It was really great. Thanks.'

'Yeah,' said Kelly. 'It was fun. Thanks, Mum.'

Finally, Nat ran out of things to say and in the silence

Mum said, 'Nearly the end of term. Are you at home for Christmas, Jack?'

'Yes, we'll be around. My nan and granddad are coming over, then we're going to my aunt and uncle the next day.'

'We'll be going to Kelly's uncle and aunt this year,' said Mum. 'They live over in Suffolk.'

Mum's hands clutched the wheel a bit tighter and her shoulders tensed.

Kelly had tried to put the visit out of her mind. She'd hardly seen Uncle John since Dad went. She'd always felt awkward with him and his family, and she was sure that John had despised Dad for not making much money.

But Dad had made beautiful things and he'd noticed everything around him. I bet he was happier. Don't suppose Uncle John has ever created anything.

She changed the subject. 'Lizzie's play this weekend. Should be great.'

Mum smiled and her shoulders relaxed. 'Yes, I'm looking forward to it – and to seeing all the scenery you painted.'

'Is Gran coming?'

'Yes. She wouldn't miss it.'

'A chance to give Lizzie a few tips, eh?'

They chatted on a bit, but all the time Kelly could sense Jack's unease. It must be horrible to think someone was following you. And now there was absolutely no doubt that this stalker would link Jack to her. She shivered suddenly and Jack turned to look at her.

'You OK?'

She nodded and moved closer to him. He put his arm round her shoulder.

She was silent for a while, then she said quietly. 'We're in this together, right?'

''Course – and Kelly, I want to ask you something.'

'What?'

'Not here. We'll talk tomorrow.'

They were still not phoning each other, and the next day there was no time to talk. During break they both had other stuff to do, and at the end of the day Mark came up to Kelly to say how much he'd enjoyed the velodrome and suggesting they did some other things together.

Only a few weeks ago, I would have been SO pleased that he even bothered to talk to me. Now, I just want him to go so I can speak to Jack!

It wasn't until Friday evening, at the first night of 'Romeo and Juliet' that they managed to snatch a few minutes together in the interval. Jack led Kelly out into the corridor, away from the buzz in the theatre.

He wasted no time. 'Your uncle and aunt,' he said.

'What about them?'

'You told me they don't live far from where your dad died.'

She nodded. 'So?'

'You don't think your uncle knows anything?'

She laughed. 'No way! He and dad were like strangers. They had nothing in common. No way would Dad confide in him.'

'Why d'you think your dad left the note and his clothes on the beach not far away from them?'

Kelly shrugged. 'I dunno. Maybe to annoy John. Maybe to send the press up there to pester John and keep them off Mum's back.'

'Umm,' said Jack.

'What?'

'It's just that … '

'What?'

'It just seems strange he should … you know, do it there … near where your uncle lives.'

Jack looked down at his hands. 'How long did you say you were going to stay in Suffolk?'

Kelly shrugged. 'A week, I think. We're going to be house-sitting for someone Uncle John knows.'

'Could you ask your mum if I can come – after Christmas.'

Kelly frowned. 'You don't want to be holed up with my family in a mouldy cottage.'

'I'd like to be with you,' he said simply. 'And we might find out more … you know … about your dad. But if you don't want me there, it's OK … '

He didn't give her a chance to answer, but went on quickly. 'I could come up by train – and bring my bike. And you could take your bike up there, too.'

'God, not bikes again! What is with you and bikes?'

He grinned. 'It's a way of getting away from other people.'

He was looking at her now and she met his eyes and nodded. 'OK,' she said slowly.

The bell went for the beginning of the next half of the show and they started walking back into the theatre.

'Don't forget to ask your mum,' he whispered.

Fourteen

When the play was over, the applause had died down and the actors had changed out of their costumes and come out of the theatre, everyone crowded round Lizzie and Mark to congratulate them. Kelly stood back and watched, seeing Lizzie animated and excited, with Mark standing beside her, not quite touching her, but you could sense the frisson between them. Every now and then their eyes would meet and they would smile.

'Don't tell me that's a "just good friends" look!' Kelly jumped. Jack had come up behind her, silently.

She smiled. 'Doesn't look that way, does it?'

She knew she'd have a chance to talk to Lizzie soon, so she gave her a quick hug of congratulations and said goodnight to Jack. She went looking for Mum and Gran, and saw Mum talking with Mark's dad. They were laughing together and then he put his arm round her shoulder.

Oh Mum!

But why shouldn't she have some fun? Dad's is dead. What's to stop her?

Gran was looking at Mum, too, then she turned quickly to Kelly. 'Well,' she said, 'for a school production, that was quite something.'

'They were great, weren't they, Mark and Lizzie?'

'Umm,' said Gran, 'there was real chemistry between them.'

A few weeks ago, I would have been so jealous, but now …

'And the sets were good, Kelly,' said Gran. 'You did a great job there.'

She rambled on about the play, the costumes and the sets, but Kelly wasn't listening.

Everything's shifting. Lizzie and Mark, Mark's dad and Mum.

She said goodnight to Jack and watched him walk away. He made her laugh, he'd taken her doubts about Dad's death seriously, he was clever. She was comfortable with him – and she trusted him. And now he was in trouble because of her.

And yes, I do feel something for him.

But she wasn't sure it was the sort of feeling she saw in the eyes of Lizzie when she smiled at Mark. Or even what she saw in Mum's eyes as she laughed at his dad's jokes.

Gran was banging on about technical aspects of the production and Kelly nodded, her eyes following Jack. He stopped to say something to Mum, and then Mark's dad was speaking. They were nodding and smiling.

He doesn't trust me to invite him to Suffolk after Christmas. I bet he's inviting himself!

'Don't you think so, Kelly?'

She focused on Gran. 'Sorry … what?'

'I knew you weren't listening. I saw you staring after that boyfriend of yours.'

'He's not really … '

Oh, what was the point? If she didn't think so now, she soon would, when she heard he'd invited himself to stay with them in Suffolk.

On the way home in the car, Mum said, 'Jack's asked if he can come and stay in Suffolk for a few days. 'Is that OK with you, Kelly? Would you like him to come?'

'Is there room?'

'Yes, it'll be a bit of a squash, but we can manage and … ' she hesitated and cleared her throat. 'Ben's offered to drive him there.'

Kelly sat up. 'Ben? Mark's dad? What about Mark and his sister?'

'Oh, they're going to their mum's for Christmas. And Ben's got friends nearby he can stay with.'

'Sounds like it's all arranged then,' said Kelly.

'No it isn't, love. Jack doesn't have to come. Only if you want him there.'

'No. It's OK. I'd like him to come – if you don't mind.'

Of course you don't mind. It's a chance to get Ben Ryley up there.

But it would be good to have a break – and for Jack, too. *Surely that man – that stalker bloke – wouldn't follow them to Suffolk?*

Kelly shivered. Were they really being followed? And was Jack right? Did it have something to do with Dad?

But why? And why now?

Suddenly Kelly felt tired of the whole thing. Tired of pursuing the clues – flimsy, cobwebby clues that never seemed to lead anywhere or reach any conclusion. It would be good to get away from home, where everything still reminded her of Dad.

The last week of term went by in a whirl of clearing up, assemblies and handing in coursework.

'If we're going to be away for Christmas, shall we forget about a tree?' asked Mum, one evening.

The Christmas Tree. Kelly and Dad had always decorated it together, putting on every single stupid bit of glittery rubbish she and Nat had made at primary school, carefully preserved from year to year. Suddenly, she felt tears coming to her eyes and Mum was immediately at her side.

'Sorry, love. That was stupid of me. Of course we'll have a tree. We'll go and get one tomorrow morning.'

But it wasn't the same. Kelly and Nat decorated it together, but there was no enthusiasm behind it. But at last it was up and the lights were winking, just like the lights in all the other houses in the street.

Mum was distracted. She was often on her phone, then switched it off when either Kelly, Gran or Nat came into the room. And sometimes Kelly would hear her chatting in her bedroom, laughing quietly, late at night.

Where's it going to lead, this thing with Ben Ryley?

Kelly went over to Lizzie's one day, the first time they'd had a real chance to talk since the play. They were sitting in Lizzie's bedroom, sorting through stuff.

'What's the deal with Mark, Lizzie?'

She looked up. 'What d'you mean?'

'You're blushing! You DO fancy him, don't you?'

'I ... well, I ... '

'So that's a yes?'

'Umm ... I ... well I got close to him during the play.'

'Not just pretend snogging, then?'

Lizzie smiled. 'No,' she said, fiddling with her hair. 'More than pretend.'

Kelly shifted over towards Lizzie and took her hand. 'I'm glad.'

'Glad?'

'Yeah. He's a great guy and you're my best friend. What's not to be glad about?'

Lizzie suddenly flung her arms round Kelly's neck. 'I thought you'd be dead upset,' she said.

'Nah. You look right together, you two.'

'And you've got Jack.'

Kelly nodded slowly. 'Yes, I s'pose.'

'And now you're inviting him up to stay with you in Suffolk. How's that gonna work, all loved-up with your family?'

'Ben Ryley's coming, too.'

'Yeah. You said. D'you think there's anything to it – this thing with him and your mum?'

Kelly shrugged. 'They knew each other at college. They go back a long way.'

'And I suppose they're both free now.'

'Yes,' said Kelly 'I s'pose. But it's a bit weird.'

'You'll have to dish the dirt when you get back.'

'LIZZIE! Enough already!'

Lizzie grinned. 'Soreee!' She punched her on the arm. 'Cheer up. You'll have a great time. You and Jack can do your own thing while your mum makes out with Ben Ryley.'

'Hmm. There's the small matter of Gran!'

'Oh yeah. I'd forgotten about her.'

'Never forget Gran,' said Kelly. 'Big mistake.'

The next few days were hectic, buying last-minute presents, deciding what to take up to Suffolk.

'Mum, what shall I get Uncle John? They've got everything.'

'I know. It's difficult. Just something you've put thought into. They don't need expensive presents.'

'Like what?'

'I dunno. Something you've made?'

'Made?'

'Would you … could you do a painting or something?' Then, seeing the look on Kelly's face, she said, 'OK. Bad idea. I understand.'

But the more Kelly thought about it, the more she liked the idea. This was something she could do. Something she was good at. She tried to remember Uncle John's house, but she'd not been there for years and her only memory was that it was very big and they had every new gadget you could imagine.

Maybe it's not such a bad idea. I could take one of Dad's

paintings out of its frame and use one of his new canvasses. There's not much time, though.

Suddenly, she was all action, finishing buying and wrapping the other presents in record time.

'Could this painting be for their whole family, Mum?'

'I don't see why not.'

She started on it that evening. She had less than a week to complete it, hardly time for it to dry. In fact it wouldn't dry if she used oils. She went up to the attic again and looked at Dad's art supplies, all carefully put away now. She dragged a set of pastels out of a draw. Dad had sometimes worked in pastels and she'd always loved what he'd done with them. She'd used them, too, and he'd always said that the medium was very forgiving, that you could rub things out, change things.

So, no canvas then. Has he still got pastel paper?

She rummaged in the attic drawers until she found some. Only a few sheets left, but she recognised the raised feel to the paper, like little tiny claws to trap the pastels and hold them fast. The sheets were quite big and she started going through Dad's paintings, but none of the frames on the ones they'd decided to get rid of was the right size. She turned to the ones they'd decided to keep.

Her favourite. His last picture – of the park and the man and the child. The frame was exactly the right size. She hesitated.

We can always reframe it, later.

Carefully, she started to take it out of its frame, slicing away the backing paper with Dad's Stanley knife, then loosening the clips. As she removed the painting, something fell out and, frowning, she picked it up.

It was a small envelope and her name was on it. In Dad's handwriting.

Her heart started to hammer in her chest and she held it between her fingers, unable to open it, afraid of what it might say.

She squatted there for ages, until her legs began aching, then, at last, she bit her lip and tore open the envelope.

A small piece of paper, something ripped from a notepad, hastily scrawled on. Seeing his writing again made her feel overwhelmingly sad and her eyes started to blur with tears. Angrily, she blinked and rubbed her eyes with her free hand, then she read what it said.

"If you find this, Kelly, I want you to know that I shall never stop loving you."

The writing was wobbly.

What a strain he had been under then. She couldn't imagine all the emotions that must have been swirling around in his head. Her heart slowed and she read it again, sniffing away the tears.

"I shall never stop loving you."

Why had he put it like that? Was she imagining it, or was that a hint to her? If he'd been intending to take his life, wouldn't he say something like, 'I *have* never stopped loving you.'

"I shall never stop loving you."

"I *shall*." The present *and the future!*

She put the note back inside the envelope and stuffed it into her pocket. She wouldn't show it to anyone else.

But it had shaken her. She took his easel, the pastel paper and the set of pastels down into her room. She couldn't start it now. She wanted to do it in natural light. She would start in the morning. And she knew exactly what she would put in it.

When Kelly went downstairs, Gran was making their tea, stirring something in a saucepan on the cooker. Nat was sitting at the table, glued to his tablet.

'Where's Mum?' asked Kelly.

'Oh, she's gone out. She won't be here for tea.'

Having a meal with Ben Ryley, I bet.

'Gran?'

'Umm.'

'This trip to Suffolk.'

For a nano-second, Gran stopped stirring. 'What about it?'

'It was Uncle John's idea, yes?'

'Yes, I think so.'

'Why d'you think he wants us there? We haven't seen him for years.'

Gran frowned. 'Maybe he wants to mend fences.'

'What do you mean?'

'Oh, nothing. But it's not good when family members quarrel, Kelly. Family is important. As you get older, you'll realise that.'

'Was there a big quarrel, then?'

Gran took the saucepan off the cooker. Her face was flushed and Kelly wasn't sure whether it was just from the heat of the cooker.

'No. Not really. It was … well, your Uncle John and your dad were very different. And,' she continued, scraping back a tendril of grey hair back behind her ear, 'we're all going to make a big effort, aren't we?'

Kelly grinned. 'Are we? Are you going to make a big effort, Gran? I know you don't like them.'

'That's enough of your cheek, Kelly Wilson. Now stop talking and set the table for me.'

Fifteen

They finally set off two days before Christmas. As they were about to get into the car, Nat wailed, 'What about my bike?'

'Don't worry love,' said Mum. 'Ben will bring it – he's got that big carrier on his car. You'll have to do without it until after Christmas, though.'

Kelly suddenly remembered what Jack had said – that she had to bring her bike, too.

'Can he bring mine too?'

'Yours?!'

Kelly flushed. 'Yeah. Jack's bringing his and we thought we could go on some rides together.'

Mum gave her a surprised look. 'You didn't say anything about this, Kelly.'

'No. Sorry. I forgot. Until now.'

Mum sighed. 'OK. I'll ring Ben.'

She got out of the car and walked back towards the house, talking into her phone, laughing.

She got back into the driving seat and started the engine. 'OK, it's all fixed. He says his rack will take them all, so that won't be a problem. Now, let's go.'

They were all tired when they finally reached the cottage. For the past two hours Nat had been asking whether they were nearly there, and Mum's patience was wearing thin. Gran had offered to do some of the driving, but Mum had curtly refused. Kelly didn't blame her; Gran drove too fast and her reactions weren't that great.

Then, at last, 'You have reached your destination,' the Satnav intoned.

It was dark when they arrived and they couldn't see much. Kelly got out of the car and stretched. She was tired and stiff. The first thing she noticed was the quiet. Although it wasn't late, there was no traffic in the village street and there were no people about. As her eyes adjusted to the darkness, she could make out the shape of the house, a long, low building set back behind a gate.

Suddenly, the door of the house opened, flooding the front garden with light.

'I thought I heard a car!'

Aunt Emma stood there, framed in the doorway, smiling, touching her beautifully-cut hair.

It was a long time since Kelly had seen her and she'd forgotten how smart she was – no wrinkles in her tight-fitting jeans and no stains on her pale cashmere top, where an expensive-looking necklace nestled.

Compared to Aunt Emma, the rest of them looked tired and scruffy, and Kelly noticed Mum pulling down her jacket and running her hand through her hair. Mum and Emma kissed awkwardly.

Gran didn't go in for any such nonsense. She plonked some cases by the door, said 'Hello Emma,' and went back to get more stuff from the car. Nat came up the path slowly, scratching his head and holding some of his things.

'Goodness, Nathan, how you've grown,' said Emma.

Nat scowled.

Then there was a bark and suddenly a large yellow dog bounded through the door and into the garden, wagging its tail and circling them joyfully.

'Tess!' cried Emma, 'I thought I'd shut you in the kitchen. Come here, you silly dog.'

But it was Kelly that the dog came to. Kelly squatted down and stroked Tess's back, then buried her nose in the dog's fur. Tess wriggled with ecstasy.

'Are there other animals, Aunt Emma?'

'Yes, dear. A couple of cats. But Tess is the one who needs attention. She loves her walks. Anyway, come in. I've got a list of instructions a mile long.'

Eventually, they all piled into the house and Emma showed them where they were to sleep and where everything was kept.

Kelly looked round the kitchen. It had a comfortable, lived-in look about it, with old beams and a tiled floor. The kitchen table was huge and solid, and there was a big old-fashioned Aga against one wall that radiated heat. She sighed and felt her shoulders drop.

Mum asked polite questions about the cousins, but Gran said nothing, standing against the Aga, her arms folded, looking at Emma.

Gran's quite scary when she's like this. I wonder what it is she's got against Emma? I thought she said we were all going to make a big effort, but she's not even trying!

When Aunt Emma had explained everything, she hovered in the doorway.

'Well, I'll leave you to it, shall I? I've put a casserole in the fridge for your dinner; it just needs warming through. Give me a ring if you need anything else.'

Mum smiled. 'That's really kind, Emma. Thanks.'

When Emma had left, Nat and Kelly went upstairs to unpack their things, but just as she was walking down the passage, Kelly heard Mum turn on Gran. 'You could have been a bit nicer to her!'

'Umm,' grunted Gran. Kelly heard Mum's exasperated sigh. 'Come on, Mum. If I can make an effort, so can you.'

Kelly walked thoughtfully up the stairs.

She started putting her clothes away. The house must be very old; the floor of the bedroom sloped and the windows were crooked, but there was plenty of space for her things. She looked at the outfit she was going to wear on Christmas Day. She'd been really pleased with it when she and Lizzie had gone shopping a few days ago. Now, she began to doubt her judgement. What would her cousin Matilda be wearing? She was all grown up now, back from uni.

I'm dreading seeing Uncle John and Matilda and Ned. What will I have to say to them?

Last of all, she took out her present. She had wrapped

up the painting very carefully. She didn't want Mum or Gran – or even Nat – to see it before she gave it to John and Emma and the others. She wanted it to be a surprise. She shivered.

Will they see what I've put in the background?

There was a scratching at the door and a whine. Kelly put the painting down.

'OK, Tess. You can come in.'

The dog bounded in and rubbed its nose around Kelly's legs.

Kelly bent down and stroked the dog's ears. 'You soppy thing.'

Later, when they were all sitting round the kitchen table eating Emma's casserole, Mum stretched and tilted her chair backwards.

'You know, I like this place,' she said. 'It's really peaceful.'

'Yeah. It's got a good feel about it,' agreed Kelly. 'What d'you think, Nat?'

'S'OK I suppose. It'll be good to go places on my bike with Jack.'

'Umm,' said Kelly. She was pretty sure that Jack wouldn't want Nat with them all the time!

She suddenly felt really tired and, as soon as they'd cleared the supper things, she took herself off to bed.

Kelly slept late the next morning and was woken by Gran drawing the curtains.

'Come on, lazybones, it's time you were up.'

Gran put a cup of tea down on the bedside table.

Kelly sat up in bed. 'What's the hurry, Gran?'

Tess pushed through the door and came up to the bed.

'What's the hurry?' said Gran, pointing at Tess. 'Have you forgotten you are supposed to be looking after that dog. And then we have to go and see the family.'

Gran's voice was flat.

'OK, OK, I'll be down in a minute.'

'And when you walk the dog, take Nat with you. He needs airing!'

Kelly smiled and took a gulp of tea.

The owners of the cottage had left directions for good dog walks, and soon Kelly and Nat were bundled up against the cold in coats and boots, and heading out the door. Kelly shoved the dog's lead in her pocket.

'Take your phone with you,' yelled Gran. 'In case you get lost.'

'As if,' muttered Kelly. 'The track leads out of the village, does a loop and comes back again. It's not rocket science.'

Nat trailed along behind her. 'Why did I have to come with you?' he said, looking up at the sky. 'It's wet and freezing and horrible.'

'Oh stop moaning, Nat. You'll like it once you've got your bike.'

'Exactly! But not going on some pointless walk.'

'It's not pointless,' snapped Kelly. 'We're exercising the dog!'

Nat didn't bother answering. He shoved his hands in his pockets and stomped on, head down.

They walked in silence for a bit, watching Tess bounding

ahead. Once, she disappeared into a wood and Kelly panicked. Her owner had said she was very obedient, but what would happen if Kelly lost her? It didn't bear thinking about.

'Tess! Tess, come here girl.'

A yellow shape disentangled itself from the undergrowth and came bounding up and sat at Kelly's feet, looking at her expectantly. Kelly dug in the pocket of her jacket and took out a dog biscuit. Tess took it without snapping.

'Good girl,' said Kelly. 'Off you go. Just as long as you come when I call.'

'What is it with you and animals?' said Nat sulkily.

'I just wish we could have a dog,' said Kelly, staring wistfully after Tess as she bounded off again. 'We could, if Gran would exercise it.'

'Can you see that happening?'

Kelly laughed. 'Not in a million years.'

The track continued to skirt the edge of the woods and Kelly and Nat walked on, heads bent against the wind and drizzle.

Kelly was lost in thought. She wondered whether she'd done the right thing in painting that picture for John and Emma.

Don't be an idiot. They won't see anything in it, they'll just see my daubs as a pretty landscape.

Dad. He was dead, she knew that, and part of her wanted to let go, accept it, like Mum and Nat. But when Jack was with her, it was different.

Jack thinks there's still some unfinished business here. The stalker, the pub.

And why did he leave that note, and his clothes, hidden

under the hut on the beach? The police said he'd died in a nearby
cave, so why ...

Nat's voice broke through her thoughts. 'I'm dreading seeing the cousins,' he muttered.

Kelly stopped and turned to him. 'I know. I feel the same. But it's been years. P'raps they've got better.'

'They just made me feel like rubbish,' muttered Nat.

Kelly kicked out at a tuft of grass on the path. 'Me too. But hey, it's Christmas. Everyone's going to have to try and be nice to each other.'

'Huh!' said Nat, scowling. Then he looked around. 'Where's the dog gone?'

'Damn,' said Kelly. 'I've not been watching her.' She looked up and down the track. 'She must have gone into the woods again.' She cupped her hands together and yelled. 'Tess! Tess! Come here girl.'

But this time there was no streak of yellow coming towards them from out of the trees. Both Kelly and Nat yelled and yelled. Kelly's heart started to beat faster.

We can't have lost her.

'We'll have to go into the woods,' she said, heading off the track and plunging into the undergrowth. Nat followed.

There was no sign of Tess.

Kelly bit her lip. 'Look, Nat. You go that way and I'll go this way. She can't have gone far, can she?'

'OK,' said Nat. 'I'll meet you back on the track.'

Kelly plunged onwards, crashing through the undergrowth. The trees grew more closely together, the further she penetrated the wood. She stopped every now and then to listen and to shout, 'Tess! Tess, come here!'

Silence.

She seemed to have been in the wood for hours and she kept imagining what might have happened to Tess. Out of breath, she sat down on a fallen log and started to cry.

Oh god. How stupid of me. I wasn't watching her. How can I even think I'm responsible enough to have a dog?

She was sitting there, her head in her hands, when suddenly she thought she heard a twig snap behind her. She whipped round.

It wasn't Tess. But she was sure someone, or something, had been there.

Don't be an idiot, Kelly. It was probably some animal. A deer or something.

But she continued to stare, unnerved.

The next moment there was a crashing sound, nothing subtle or eerie about it, and Tess was at her side.

Tess's nose was covered in dirt and Kelly sobbed with relief, half-crying, half-laughing, flinging her arms round the dog's neck. Tess rubbed herself against Kelly, then sat at her feet, expecting a treat.

'Oh no,' said Kelly, wiping her eyes and digging in her pocket for the lead. 'You don't get a treat for running away.'

She attached the lead and headed out of the woods. 'Nat,' she yelled, 'I've got her.'

Nat was already back on the track, looking cold and miserable.

'Can we go now?'

Kelly nodded. 'It's not far.'

Just as they were coming into the village from the other end, Kelly stopped and pointed.

'I think that's Uncle John's house,' she said.

'What, that big posh one?'

She nodded. 'I think so. I can't be certain, but it looks sort of familiar.'

Nat's shoulders drooped.

Sixteen

Later that morning, they all trailed up the road to Uncle John's house. No one said much as they stood on the front doorstep and waited for the big front door to open.

Inside, they sat round the big table in the kitchen and had coffee while the family Labrador snuffled about looking for pats and tidbits. Kelly didn't say much, but she realised that a lot of what she'd remembered about Uncle John wasn't quite true. Dad, Mum and Gran had been so critical of him, but he wasn't as bossy as she'd remembered. Or maybe he'd changed. And he had a look of Dad about him, which she found spooky.

Emma fussed around, making sure they had all they needed, then she perched her immaculate slim body on the Aga rail, sipping her coffee.

Matilda (or Tilly, as the family called her) was still as tall and as beautiful as Kelly remembered, but she was no longer that supercilious sixteen-year-old who had made Kelly feel so insignificant. Uni had obviously knocked a few of the sharp edges off her, and she seemed much more relaxed and genuinely friendly. She asked about school and stuff, and then she said something that took Kelly by surprise.

'I remember you as this gawky kid, Kelly, but you've turned out really lovely.'

Kelly blushed to the roots of her red hair. 'What?' she said, laughing, 'With my wild red hair and freckles! You *have* to be joking!'

Tilly shook her head. 'No, honest, your hair is such a great colour – *and* you've got curls. I'm so jealous. And your features are terrific. You're like a Botticelli painting (Tilly was studying History of Art). Has anyone ever painted you?'

Kelly's face was still flushed. She hung her head. 'Only Dad,' she said quietly. 'And that was ages ago.'

Tilly put her hand on Kelly's arm. 'I'm sorry, that was tactless.'

'Doesn't matter,' mumbled Kelly.

They went on then to talk about other stuff, about Tilly's friends at uni, what she was going to do when she left, about boyfriends.

'Mum says your boyfriend's coming here after Christmas.'

Kelly shook her head. 'Jack? Oh, he's not really a boyfriend. Just a mate from school.'

Tilly raised her eyebrows but didn't comment.

During a gap in the conversation, Kelly looked around her. Mum, John and Emma all seemed to be getting on OK, but she noticed how Gran had placed herself as far away from

John as possible. And Ned had obviously run out of things to say to Nat. Kelly turned in their direction.

'Nat, did you tell Ned about our trip to the velodrome?'

Suddenly Ned's eyes lit up. He could talk sport for ever – any sport – and Nat finally found his voice and started telling him about his bike, the velodrome and that Jack was coming with his ace bike and they were going to take off and explore.

'I'll come with you,' said Ned. 'Show you where to go.'

Oh god, this is suddenly turning into some crowded bike ride. Jack won't want Nat with us – and certainly not Ned.

Before they left, Kelly excused herself and went to the loo, looking carefully at the sorts of pictures hanging on the walls in the hall. A lot of them were modern and probably very expensive. She liked what she saw and she knew that Dad would have liked them too.

My picture could fit in quite well here. If they want it.

They said their goodbyes and walked back through the village to the cottage.

Mum took Kelly's arm. 'That went really well,' she said, and Kelly could hear the relief in her voice.

'Yeah, they're not so bad after all. I'm glad we've come.'

Gran said nothing. She walked in front, stony-faced.

They had brought a tiny, fake Christmas tree with them, together with a few miniature decorations and lights, and Kelly put it up in the lounge window and opened the curtains slightly so that it could be seen from the street outside. They lit the fire and it was soon a roaring blaze.

Mum sat down in front of the fire, stretched out her legs and wriggled off her shoes.

'This is nice,' she said.

'Our first Christmas away from home,' said Kelly.

Mum nodded.

No one needed to say anything else. They all had their thoughts. Kelly smiled as she watched Tess push her way to the front and flop down as close to the fire as possible.

It was Tess who woke Kelly on Christmas morning, shoving a wet nose into her armpit. Kelly put out a hand to stroke the dog, then rolled over to look at the clock on her bedside table.

'It's only seven o'clock, Tess. Give me a break!'

But Tess started to whine and wouldn't go away.

At last Kelly heaved herself out of bed. She pushed her feet into her slippers and, rubbing her eyes and yawning, crept downstairs. Tess scraped at the back door and Kelly let her out into the garden.

As she stood in the kitchen window watching Tess snuffle in the back garden and then squat on the lawn, she thought about yesterday, about what had happened in the woods. Had there really been someone there?

I wasn't looking for anyone, or expecting anyone, yet I'm sure there was someone there.

Even now, she had a prickling sensation at the back of her neck, remembering that feeling of being watched.

She let Tess back into the kitchen and fed her.

'Happy Christmas, Tess,' she said, stroking the dog's ears.

She made herself a drink and was about to go upstairs again, when Gran came into the kitchen.

'Hello love. Happy Christmas.'

Kelly smiled at her and suddenly hugged her.

'Hey, what was that for?'

'A Christmas hug,' said Kelly.

'Want a cuppa?' asked Kelly, and Gran nodded.

They sat at the kitchen table. Gran sighed. 'It seems all wrong, not being busy with the Christmas dinner,' she said.

'But it's nice for you to have a break, isn't it?'

Gran gave a non-commital grunt.

'Mum did offer to make the puddings or do some of the veg,' said Kelly. 'But Aunt Emma said it was all under control.'

'No doubt,' said Gran flatly.

'Come on, Gran. It was OK yesterday. And Tilly and Ned were fine.'

'Oh yes, the young ones were fine,' said Gran.

There was a loaded silence. Then Kelly decided to pose the question she'd often wanted to ask.

'What is it about Uncle John, Gran? Why do you hate him?'

Gran's head jerked up. '*Hate* him? Of course I don't hate him.'

'Well, you gave a pretty good imitation of hating him yesterday. You didn't speak a word to him.'

'Nor him to me,' retorted Gran.

'Oh, for heaven's sake,' muttered Kelly, scraping back her chair, but Gran put a hand on her arm.

'Don't let's fall out on Christmas Day,' she said. 'Perhaps I should have made more effort, but it's just that ... '

'What?'

'I think he could have helped your mum a lot more when … '

'When Dad disappeared?'

Gran nodded. 'He never came to the house once,' she said. 'Never phoned, never wrote. It would have made a difference, you know – to Mum – to know he was thinking of her.'

'Maybe he was sad, too,' said Kelly quietly.

'Huh!' said Gran. 'That man has only ever thought of himself and his own.'

Kelly said nothing.

Later in the morning they all trailed over to Uncle John's house, clutching bags of presents. Kelly had put on her new dress and she'd made a real effort with her hair and make-up.

'Wow!' said Mum. 'You look so grown-up! That really suits you, Kell.'

And even Gran nodded approval.

As they walked up the drive to Uncle John's house, Kelly started feeling seriously nervous.

'When do you think we'll unwrap the presents, Mum?'

Mum smiled. 'You sound like a ten-year-old! Can't wait, eh?'

'No, just wondered. They may do it differently.'

'Well, Emma said we'd have drinks and presents first, then eat later.'

'OK.'

Kelly had to admit, when they went in through the front

door, that everything looked lovely. The decorations, the fire in the big front room, the huge Christmas tree, all tastefully decorated, the pile of presents under the tree. For a moment, she felt as if she was in the pages of some magazine, looking at the perfect family Christmas.

There was a loud pop as Uncle John opened a bottle of Champagne and poured it into their glasses.

He brought one to Kelly. 'I'm not sure,' she said, looking at Mum.

Mum smiled. 'Just a little glass,' she said. 'As it's Christmas.'

Kelly took a sip and the bubbles tickled her nose. She spluttered as she took a sip and swallowed it.

Tilly was handing round canapés. She came up to Kelly.

'Wow, are these home-made?' asked Kelly.

'No way! Far too much hassle!'

Kelly relaxed a little and Tilly continued to stand beside her. 'You look great, Kelly,' she said. 'That dress really suits you.'

Kelly looked anxiously at Tilly. 'It's not too much?' Tilly didn't appear to have made a huge effort. She was wearing a long top and leggings, but she still managed to look amazing.

'No. It's great. Really.'

'All right,' said Uncle John, a little later. 'Time for presents.'

There was obviously a well-rehearsed routine to their Christmas Day and Tilly and Ned leapt into action, reading labels and dishing out the parcels. They all sat around, opening their presents.

Every now and again, Kelly glanced over at Gran. She

was sitting on the sofa next to Mum and, although she hadn't been saying much, the Champagne seemed to have relaxed her a little and at least she wasn't scowling.

When Tilly dug out Kelly's present for Uncle John and the family from the pile, Kelly said quickly, 'I hope it's OK. It's for all of you.'

But she had to wait for an agonising few minutes before Uncle John and Aunt Emma carefully unwrapped it.

Uncle John held it away from him, squinting.

'It's really lovely, Kelly,' said Emma. She took it from John and put it on the mantelpiece over the fire. Uncle John came over to Kelly and kissed her.

'You've inherited your father's talent,' he said quietly. 'We'll treasure it.'

The rest of the day went well. The food was amazing, as Kelly knew it would be, and Gran had thawed out, even though she'd been swamped with presents of bath oils and the sort of stuff she never used. Kelly couldn't help smiling when Gran was struggling to be enthusiastic about yet another bottle which would almost certainly find its way to a local bric-a-brac stall when they returned home. She caught Gran's eye and grinned at her.

John and Emma had given Kelly some expensive clothes. They were lovely, but she wasn't sure when she'd ever wear them. And Nat had been overwhelmed with gear for his bike. His enthusiasm for his presents was genuine; just as well, as he was a rubbish actor.

At the end of the day, full of good food, they finally said their goodbyes, but just as they were leaving, Gran went to look at Kelly's painting. Kelly watched.

At first, Gran stood there, her arms folded, smiling approvingly, but suddenly she tensed and leaned forward, peering at what Kelly had put in the far distance. She gave a gasp and spun round, almost tripping in her eagerness to put some distance between herself and the painting.

As Gran walked quickly towards the door, she caught Kelly's eye and Kelly returned her glance without flinching.

Seventeen

The next morning they had a late breakfast. Nat was quite excited (for him) at the thought of putting all his new gear on his bike, and he kept asking when Jack would be arriving.

'I told you,' said Kelly crossly. 'Some time tomorrow.'

Mum was really relaxed. 'You know, I'd been dreading Christmas Day,' she confided to Kelly as they made toast. 'But it was really good. I'm glad we came.'

'Me too,' said Kelly.

Gran went out of her way to avoid speaking to Kelly except when really necessary, and when Kelly got ready to walk the dog, she looked relieved.

'Want to come, Nat?' asked Kelly.

He shook his head and Kelly took the lead, called the dog and headed outside.

This time, she went through the village and then onto the

track, so that she had a good view of Uncle John's house. There, she stood still, stamping her feet and banging her hands together to keep warm, looking across at the house. Tess whined.

Kelly was about to walk on when she saw Gran's figure, striding up the drive to John's house.

What's she doing? Why's she going up there on her own?

Kelly waited until she saw that Gran had gone into the house, then she let Tess off the lead and they continued their walk.

'And this time, Tess, don't you dare try any tricks. I'll be watching you all the time!'

Kelly kept a careful eye on the dog, making her come back when she looked like disappearing into the woods, but all the time she was wondering why Gran had gone up to Uncle John's house.

Kelly couldn't wait for Jack to arrive.

He's got under your skin, Kelly Wilson.

Just another twenty-four hours to get through. But then Ben Ryley would be here too, and she wasn't sure how she felt about that.

When Kelly got back to the cottage, Gran was still out. Kelly sat around with Mum. They talked about John and Emma, and Tilly and Ned, about what a good day they'd had yesterday.

'That was a lovely picture you did for them,' said Mum. 'I could see it meant a lot that you made such an effort.'

Kelly looked up. Mum had noticed nothing in the picture, then.

At last, Mum rose to her feet and stretched. 'I'll make us a sandwich,' she said.

'Is Gran coming back for lunch?'

Mum frowned and looked at her watch. 'She's been out for ages. I hope she's OK. I'll give her a ring.'

There were several rings before Gran answered her mobile.

'You OK? Will you be back for lunch? It doesn't matter if not, I'm only doing a bowl of soup and a sandwich.'

Kelly watched as Mum nodded at the phone, frowning. 'OK, fine. We'll see you later.'

'She's not coming back?'

Mum shook her head. 'She's staying for lunch with John and Emma,' she said.

'Wow! That's a turn-up for the books,' said Kelly.

Mum started filling sandwiches. 'Umm,' she said.

Nat had been playing on a new game, but hunger drove him into the kitchen and he picked up a sandwich and started eating. Then his phone rang and his whole face lit up.

'Yeah. Yeah, that's great. I'll be with you in a bit.'

'That was Ned,' he said. 'He's got this ace new game – and he wants to show me his bike and stuff.'

'Great,' said Mum and Kelly in unison, as Nat headed for the door.

'Sit down, Nat. Finish your lunch first.'

When he'd left, Mum said, 'That's kind of Ned.' There was a pause. 'Why don't you give Tilly a ring, maybe do something with her?'

Kelly hesitated.

I'm not sure I want to go up to the house if Gran's there.

'Tell you what, Mum. Why don't we go out for a drive, just you and me. We could take the dog and have a look round.'

Mum frowned briefly. ' OK, ' she said, slowly, 'if that's what you'd like.'

Kelly's phone rang and Lizzie's name came up on the screen.

'Hi!'

'Hi yourself,' said Lizzie. 'How's it going up there in the sticks? When does lover-boy arrive?'

They chatted on, laughed and joked and talked about their Christmas Day. When Kelly ended the call, she stood there for a moment, still staring at the screen.

Kelly didn't see Gran for the rest of the day. John and Emma were going out with friends that evening and had invited Gran along, so she didn't get back to the cottage until late, by which time Kelly was in her bedroom.

She's avoiding me.

The next morning, Gran stayed in her room, saying she had a headache, and by the time Kelly came back from walking the dog, Gran had disappeared again.

Jack and Mark's dad were due at lunchtime, and Mum was fussing about, making up a bed for Jack and cooking something special. Kelly watched her.

She looks so excited.

But it hurt, all the same.

Then, at last, a car drew up outside the cottage, bristling with bikes, and Ben Ryley and Jack tumbled out.

As Jack unloaded the bikes, Nat was full of questions, showing him his new gear and talking about Ned's super bike.

'Hey, give him a chance, Nat,' said Mum, smiling.

At last, after lunch, Jack and Kelly had a chance to talk. Ben had taken Mum off to meet the friends he'd be staying with, Gran was still with Uncle John, and Ned had phoned and asked Nat to go for a ride.

The cottage was suddenly silent with secrets.

Jack and Kelly watched as the others left, then turned to each other.

'So?' said Jack.

Kelly sat down suddenly. 'I've done something stupid.'

Jack frowned and Kelly went on, telling him about her painting and what she'd put in it, telling him of Gran's reaction and how Gran had been avoiding her ever since.

'Wow!' said Jack. 'Do you think she'll say anything about it?'

Kelly started chewing her fingers. 'I dunno. But she's suddenly spending a lot of time with my uncle. It's really weird.'

'You don't think your uncle knows something?'

Kelly frowned. 'I doubt it.'

'Do you think your Gran knows something more about your dad than she's letting on?'

Kelly nodded. 'I've always thought that. Anyway,' she said, 'let's forget about about my family and go biking.'

'What! Did I hear you correctly, Kelly Wilson?'

She smiled. 'You'd like that wouldn't you? And … and I'd like to go over to Dunwich. To that beach where Dad … '

'Really? You sure?'

She nodded. 'Umm. While it's just the two of us. Without Nat tagging along.'

'OK,' he said slowly, putting out his hand and dragging her up, holding her briefly and then releasing her. 'Let's go.

There's only a couple more hours of daylight. We'll have to hurry.'

She nodded.

A few minutes later, wrapped up against the raw wind that blew in from the sea, they were on their bikes, riding as fast as they could towards the coast, Kelly wearing her new helmet.

They'd only gone a mile and already Kelly was puffed.

'I've got to rest for a bit,' she yelled.

Jack turned back and rode up to her. 'We've still got a way to go. Are you sure you want to do this now?'

'We're only up here a few days, Jack. We might not have another chance to be on our own.'

'OK. Let me know when you're good to go.'

They set off again, Jack leading the way. He flew down small lanes, never hesitating. Kelly struggled to keep up, but it was her idea. She was determined to make the journey.

Suddenly they saw a signpost. 'Dunwich.'

Kelly stopped dead. Ahead of her, Jack's brakes screeched and he turned and rode back.

'You OK?' he asked, when he reached her.

'It's … I dunno. It's just seeing the name.'

Jack flung down his bike and came over to her.

'We don't have to go there,' he said. 'We can go back.'

Suddenly Kelly put her arms round his neck and reached up and kissed him.

A proper kiss, even though her helmet got in the way.

When at last he let her go, she was trembling.

'Kelly,' he said.

'Let's go,' she said quietly.

Jack touched her cheek with his hand.

They rode into the village, down the only street, and headed for the beach. There was a little café and a pub in the street, and scrubby grass-tufted dunes that led down to a pebbly beach. Further along, they could see cliffs. They left the bikes behind a gorse bush on the dunes and walked onto the beach.

'It's such a little place,' said Kelly.

'Wasn't always,' said Jack. 'I googled it. It was once a huge port.'

'What?'

He nodded. 'In medieval times it was as big as London.'

Kelly frowned. 'So what happened?'

'Erosion, apparently. And some huge storms.'

'What, so the town sort of fell into the sea?'

'I guess.'

Kelly shivered. She tried to imagine her dad here, but she couldn't. She couldn't explain, either, why she felt that he had never left that note and his clothes weighed down with a stone, under the hut further down the beach, as the Press had said.

Why? Why had he gone into a cave to die? A cave with such a hidden entrance that no one knew about it. So how had Dad known about it?

They took off their bike helmets and sat together, looking out at the dull wintery sea. There was someone walking a dog along the beach, but apart from that, the place was deserted.

Jack looked around. 'It's so quiet and empty.' He reached for her again and this time their kiss lasted a long time.

When, at last, they parted, the dog walker was closer and

Kelly saw that he was talking into his phone. She screwed up her eyes and ran her hand through her windswept hair.

'That man,' she said, nudging Jack. 'Have you seen him before?'

Jack followed her gaze. He frowned. 'No. Why?'

'I dunno. I'm just feeling a bit spooked. I thought he might be … you know, the guy who's been stalking you … '

Jack laughed. 'No. He's just walking his dog, that's all.'

Jack looked up at the sky. 'We'd better go,' he said. 'It's getting dark. I'll just run up and see if the café's open. I'll get some drinks if it is.'

Kelly continued to sit looking out to sea. She felt stiff and cold and sore. Maybe this hadn't been such a good idea. She felt absolutely no connection with this place. If Dad had died here, surely she should feel *something*.

Then she smiled. Perhaps, kissing Jack here, the place had lost its horror for her. From now on, she'd remember it for that.

He's dead. I must stop this. Gran's stressed because of what I put in that picture. Why did I do that? What an idiot.

She shivered and turned round to look behind her at the village café. Jack's bike was leaning against the wall outside.

He's been ages. What's he doing in there? It's starting to get really dark.

She got up stiffly and collected her bike. As she wheeled it up towards the café, the man on the beach watched her, then he spoke into his phone again, put it back in his pocket and continued walking his dog.

She leaned her bike up against the wall, beside Jack's, and tried to open the door of the café. It was locked and she saw a sign saying 'Closed' in the window. She frowned. She ran round to the back of the building, but there was no one there. Why should there be? It was December, for goodness sake, and it was cold. Who would be there just after Christmas? Anyone with any sense would be at home, in the warm.

She yelled out. 'Jack! Where are you?'

There was no answer, just the sudden screech of a seagull.

She jumped, suddenly feeling really scared. Too bad he'd said they shouldn't phone each other. She needed to know where he was. She dragged her phone from her pocket and frowned at it. She could swear she'd left it on, but the screen was dark. She stabbed at it.

Nothing. It was dead. She couldn't understand it. She'd charged it recently. It wasn't even saying there was no signal. It was just blank.

She noticed the pub. Maybe he'd gone there. She ran down the street and banged on the door, but there was no answer. It, too, was closed and empty.

The whole place was deserted.

She was alone. It was getting dark and she had no way of getting in touch – with Jack, with Mum, with anyone.

She looked all over. At first just walking up and down, but then running everywhere, breathless, stopping to shout out Jack's name at intervals. He wouldn't desert her like this, would he? Not Jack? And anyway, where could he go without his bike?

She ran back to the beach and looked up and down. But there was no one. The man and his dog had gone. She could feel her heart pumping away in her chest.

She was crying now, great gulping sobs.

Stop it, Kelly. Think. Something's happened to Jack. He might be hurt.

She looked up at the sky, the darkness closing in. She'd have to ride back and get help.

She shouted out a few more times, her voice hoarse, but there was no reply.

Nothing.

She mounted her bike, strapping on her new helmet with fumbling fingers, wobbling and gulping down her sobs. At least she had a light. And as soon as she saw anyone, she would stop and ask to use their phone.

She set off, back the way they'd come. At first the road was easy, but then the bit she was dreading, the road through the woods. The dark was enveloping her here and only the beam of the bike light cut weakly through it.

She was pedalling as hard as she could, but her legs ached with tiredness and there was still a long way to go. Once she heard the eerie sound of an owl hooting and she nearly fell off her bike.

What's happened to Jack? Where is he? He wouldn't leave me.

She stopped for a few precious moments to get her breath, balancing with one foot on the ground. It was then that she heard the sound. It was coming from the woods, from somewhere in front of her. The sound of twigs snapping and a heavy tread with no attempt at concealment.

She scraped her knee in her hurry to get back on the bike. She saw a light and whoever was holding it was running now, crashing towards her. Someone heavy, big.

She started pedalling harder, the adrenalin pumping her

legs, but it was too late, she had no time to get up speed before her path was blocked.

Eighteen

Jack was in a car which was racing down the little country roads at breakneck speed. He was being flung from one side to the other as the car screeched round corners. At the same time he was struggling against the tape over his mouth and trying to release his hands, which were tied behind his back.

It had all happened so fast. One moment he'd been rattling the door of the village café, desperate for a drink and furious that it was shut, and the next he'd been grabbed violently from behind. He'd tried to cry out, but as he'd taken a breath to scream, he'd been kneed in the back, making him fall on the ground, and this was when his hands were tied and his mouth taped. His phone had fallen out of his pocket and the person standing over him had kicked it away into the bushes.

Then he'd been dragged into a waiting car.

He was still in shock, his breathing fast and shallow and

his gut twisting with fear. He forced himself to take deeper breaths, trying to calm himself, to stop his knees from shaking. The driver didn't look at him; the man had his eyes on the road, but Jack knew who it was. The man from the pub. The guy who had spilt the drink and who had followed him to the velodrome.

He had recognised him at once. The thick-set body, dark hair and beard.

What does he want with me? Who is he? Where's he taking me?

Jack tried to say something, but he couldn't speak through the tape and only managed a moan. He shut his eyes. He had no idea where they were going and he felt sick. Who was this maniac? He tried to fight down his panic.

The journey seemed to last for ever, but at last the car slowed down. Jack opened his eyes and saw that they were driving through a small town. The man was stopping for some traffic lights.

Jack lunged towards the door and tried to open it with his tied hands, banging uselessly at the handle.

For the first time, the driver spoke. 'The door's locked.'

Jack's head jerked up.

The man seemed to read his mind. 'You don't need to know who I am. Just keep quiet. I'm not going to hurt you; I only want to ask you some questions.'

And then, in one movement, he suddenly leaned over, pulled something out of the glove compartment and fitted it over Jack's eyes. Jack wasn't expecting it and was taken by surprise. The mask was very tight and, although he tried to tear it off, it was impossible with his tied hands.

'It will not be for long,' said the man. 'Once we are inside, I will remove it.'

Jack registered the slight formality in the man's speech.

He's not English.

After more useless struggling, Jack gave up and leaned back into the seat.

What would Kelly do? What would she think when she found his bike?

Perhaps by now she had phoned for help, and people would be looking for him. He held onto the thought.

He felt the car turn and slow down, then stop, but the engine continued running and he heard the sound of the man's fingers drumming on the steering wheel, then a slight mechanical creaking. He recognised it as an overhead automatic garage door opening up. It sounded just like the one they had at home. A few moments later, the car was driven slowly through, presumably into a garage. Once again Jack scrabbled at the door, but the man didn't move.

He's waiting until the door closes. He thinks I'll make a run for it.

There was a faint clunk as the garage door slid down into place and Jack felt the man undo his seat belt.

'All right, you can get out now.' He leant over Jack and yanked off the mask, pulling strands of Jack's hair as he did so. Jack flinched. The man heaved himself out of the driver's seat and came round the car to let Jack out.

As Jack climbed out of the car he looked around, but there were no clues here. It was all so ordinary. A featureless, ordinary modern garage, with all the things you'd expect to see in a garage. Tins of paint, electrical equipment, a mower, jump leads. He saw it all in a blur of fear as the man took his arm and propelled him through a door into the house.

Again, an ordinary, modern house. The man switched on some lights and Jack noticed that all the curtains had already been closed. So no one could see in.

The place felt unlived in, sterile. Who did it belong to?

'Sit down, Jack.' It was an order.

How does he know my name?

'I will take off the tape,' said the man. 'But if you do anything stupid, you will regret it.'

Again, that foreignness in the way he spoke. And the voice calm and controlling.

He's threatening me. If I scream for help, he'll hit me. This guy means business.

The man seemed to be waiting for some sort of answer, so Jack nodded, then winced with pain as the tape was ripped from his mouth. Jack's eyes watered and he could feel a trickle going down his chin. He licked it and tasted blood.

Bastard. How dare he do this to me.

The man sat down opposite him.

Jack was still licking his lips. 'I need a drink,' he said, his voice hoarse.

The man's eyes flickered. For a moment, Jack thought the man was going to hit him, but he obviously thought better of it and heaved himself up from the chair and went over to the sink, his eyes constantly darting back towards Jack.

He wasn't familiar with the place, that was obvious. He opened several cupboards before he found a glass. His hand hovered over it and then he selected a plastic beaker instead.

He thinks I'd break the glass and attack him with it, sick bastard.

There was a spluttering as the water came out of the cold tap, as if no one had turned it on for some time.

Before he handed Jack the water, he took out a knife from a drawer and, for a terrifying moment, Jack thought he was going to stab him. He instinctively recoiled when the man approached him, but he simply sliced through the plastic ties around Jack's hands. He didn't replace the knife in the drawer, but laid it down beside him on the table.

Jack rubbed his wrists, then took the beaker of water and gulped it down as the man stared at him from across the table.

'Who are you? Why have you brought me here?' said Jack, hoping he didn't sound as scared as he felt.

The man glanced at his watch. 'We have very little time,' he said. 'What does your father know about Stephen Wilson?'

'*What!?*'

Jack was completely thrown. What did his dad have to do with anything?

'I don't know what you're talking about,' he began, 'My dad … '

But he got no further. The man stood up and slapped Jack hard across the face. Jack cried out and reeled back from the force of the blow.

'I have no time for lies,' said the man, as Jack sat with tears pouring down his face, his hand to his cheek.

Jack began to shake. 'I'm sorry,' he stuttered, though he didn't know what he was apologising for.

'That's better.' The man leant back in his chair. He picked up the knife and balanced it in his hand.

'Your father worked on the local newspaper when Stephen Wilson disappeared.'

It was a statement, not a question. Jack nodded.

'And now he works for a national paper.' Jack swallowed nervously and nodded again, unsure where this was going.

'He knows that Stephen Wilson did not die.'

'But they found his remains ... '

The man ignored him and carried on. 'Stephen Wilson worked as a special kind of agent. A secret agent. Do you think that we are deceived by a press report saying that his remains have been found?'

Jack didn't answer. It was too much to take in.

'Your father, also, he knows this. He is on his trail. And he is using you to get to him.'

'What! No, my dad would never do that!'

The man laughed harshly and then suddenly slammed his hand down on the table. Jack jumped.

'You pretend to be an an innocent boy, eh?' he said. 'Your father, he is encouraging your friendship with the girl, with the family. We know what he is doing. He's a journalist, after a big story. You have been very clever, pretending you care for the girl, getting secrets from her. She thinks her father is still alive. We *know* he is still alive.'

'She *doesn't*,' said Jack. 'None of them believe he's still alive.' He hated the way his voice was trembling.

The man took no notice. 'I think your father knows where he is and I need to know, too. And I need to know quickly. Before Stephen Wilson disappears again.'

'Why?' said Jack. 'I don't understand. Even if he was alive, why do you ... '

The man picked up the knife again. Its blade flashed as it caught the light.

'Revenge,' he said.

'What for?' whispered Jack.

'Stephen Wilson has caused us a lot of trouble in the past. Four years ago, we found out what he had been doing and who he was. And that was when he disappeared.'

'He took his own life,' muttered Jack.

The man shifted in his seat and Jack flinched. 'That's what we thought. Until a few weeks ago, when certain information came our way.'

'What do you mean?'

The man leaned back in his chair and narrowed his eyes. 'The organisation he worked for.' He hesitated. 'It is very secret. All undercover. But we know about it. And now we have a contact in it.'

Suddenly the man leaned forward again, his elbows on the table, looking straight at Jack. 'We know that Stephen Wilson is somewhere up here, somewhere near his brother's house, and when you got yourself invited up here, that confirmed it for us. Your father knows where he is, doesn't he? He knows that Stephen Wilson is here to see his family one last time before he vanishes. We were waiting for your father to lead us to him, but we can't wait any longer. The family will soon go home and our chance to find him will go too.'

The man laughed. It was a harsh, humourless sound. 'We know your father's game. He is a top journalist. He is following a top story, isn't he? Can you imagine the scoop, eh? A man risen from the dead!'

'My dad has nothing … ' began Jack, then he recoiled as the man lunged forward again, the knife in his hand.

'Don't lie to me, you stupid boy.'

Suddenly an image of Kelly flashed through Jack's mind.

'His family believed the police,' he said. 'They think he's dead. If he suddenly appeared … '

'Don't pretend to be stupid. Stephen Wilson wouldn't come out of hiding to meet up with his family. The organisation will just let him catch sight of them, see that they are well, before he disappears from their life for ever.

Jack sat, stunned. All he knew was that this guy had got it completely wrong. Jack was certain that his dad had nothing to do with this. He'd told him to keep well out of it, hadn't he?

The man was still holding the knife and his phone rang, making Jack jump. With his eyes still on Jack, he took the phone from his pocket. He spoke briefly – and not in a language that Jack understood.

'Good,' he said, snapping his phone shut. 'My people have contacted your father. He knows we have you. He'll soon talk.' He stood up scraping his chair back and fingering the blade of the knife again. 'He won't want to see his boy hurt, will he?'

Nineteen

Kelly screamed, then she took a breath to scream again, but felt a large hand over her mouth and heard a man's voice. She was so scared she couldn't take in what he was saying. She struggled and kicked, and she heard the man swear. She twisted round to try and free herself, but she couldn't. She was held firm.

'For heaven's sake, Kelly, calm down. It's me, Uncle John.'

His voice was even, if a bit breathless.

'What are you doing? Let me go!'

'OK. OK. I didn't want you screaming the place down. My truck's parked up the track. I'll take you back.'

He released her then, but she backed away.

'I'll bike back on my own. I don't want a lift.'

'Don't be silly. You can't take Jack's bike back, can you? I'll put both bikes in the truck and we'll be back in no time.'

'Where is Jack?'

'We know where he is. No need to worry.'

'What are you doing here?' she asked.

He didn't answer. 'Come on, the truck's just back up here.'

She stood, confused. Why was he here? And where was Jack? And how did Uncle John know what had happened to him? But she couldn't get away from him now, so she sighed and stumbled after him. She hadn't noticed that there was a wide track leading off the road. His truck was parked not far away and he opened the passenger door for her to get in, then he drove back to the road, loaded up her bike, then drove back into Dunwich and collected Jack's bike.

It was completely dark now and Kelly's head was in such a muddle that it was only some time after they'd left Dunwich that she realised that they was driving in the wrong direction.

'This isn't the way back to the village,' she said.

John didn't answer. Kelly tried to open the passenger door but it was locked.

Uncle John was driving, fast, his face grim.

'Where are you taking me? What are you doing?'

'I'm taking you somewhere where we can talk, Kelly.'

Kelly's heart was beating very fast. Surely he wouldn't harm her, would he? He was her uncle for goodness sake.

'Jack'll worry about me. What's happening to him? How do you know he's safe? Where's he gone? Why did he disappear like that?'

John sighed. 'Nothing bad will happen to him.'

'How do you know? Why … ?'

John cut her off. 'That's enough questions, Kelly. It's you and Jack we need answers from.'

'*We?* What do you mean, *"we"*? Who?'

He didn't answer.

They drove in silence for a long time, but at last the car slowed down and Uncle John parked in the road, beside a small, isolated cottage. There was a light on in the window.

John got out and opened the passenger door.

'Come on, Kelly,' he said, and his voice was quite gentle, but still her legs were like jelly, and not only from all the biking she'd done that day.

She looked round desperately, but they were miles from anywhere. She'd no idea where she was. She dragged her phone out of her pocket. John looked at it.

'It won't work, Kelly. It's been blocked,' he said. 'You can't use it just now.'

She stared at him. 'What do you mean, *blocked?* How? Who did that? Mum will worry ... '

'I've already phoned your mum,' said John. 'I've told her you and Jack are with me.'

'But that's a lie! Where is he?'

John didn't bother replying. He opened the front door of the cottage and ushered Kelly inside.

'I need the toilet,' she said.

'OK,' said John, slowly. He showed her where it was and stood in the passage outside.

She was so tense, it took her ages to go and she looked round the small downstairs toilet to distract herself. She noticed that there was a razor and some washing things on the shelf by the sink. So, someone was living here. There was no window, so no way out, but even if she escaped, where would she go? Her phone was useless and she had no idea where she was.

John's face was unreadable. He didn't smile at her, but pointed down the passage.

'In here,' he said curtly, leading the way into a small sitting room. He waited until she was inside, then he closed the door. Kelly looked around. There was a fire burning in the grate, but only one light – a standard lamp beside a big armchair. Apart from the pool of light from this, and the glow from the fire, the room was in darkness.

'Why have you brought me here? Who lives here?' Her voice was squeaky.

John drew up another, high-backed, chair and placed it across from the big armchair.

'Sit down,' he said.

'I ... I don't want ... '

'Sit *down*!'

Feeling very small and scared, Kelly obeyed. John stared at her for a few moments, then he lowered himself into the big armchair and they looked at each other in the gloom, the flames from the fire occasionally leaping up and casting patterns of light on the walls.

'Where are we?' said Kelly.

John ignored the question. He leant forward, clasping his hands round his knees. 'I'm going to ask the questions, Kelly, not you.'

There was complete silence for a few moments and Kelly felt a wave of nausea in her stomach.

'I want to know, Kelly,' he said at last, 'What you and your friend Jack have been doing.'

'What do you mean ... ?' she began, but he interrupted, angrily.

'You know exactly what I mean,' he said.

'I ... well, I've, we've ... ' she began.

'Take your time,' said John. 'I'm in no hurry and I want to hear it in your own words.'

Kelly swallowed. She was so confused. She had no idea whether she should trust him or not. Had he done something to Jack?

And then she started to cry. It came out of nowhere and she couldn't stop. Great heaving sobs, her whole body trembling from fatigue, from fear.

What's going to happen to me? What's happened to Jack?

John said nothing. At one point he got up and fetched a box of tissues and handed it to her. He didn't try and comfort her.

Finally, she blew her nose and wiped her eyes, balling up the damp tissues in her hands.

She looked at John and he met her eyes, unflinchingly.

'I just never believed that Dad was dead.'

Her voice was no more than a whisper and John made her repeat what she'd said.

'Why?' he asked, but his voice was gentler now. 'They found that note and his clothes on the beach. And then later his ... his remains.'

She took a deep breath. 'Because I saw him,' she said.

John's head jerked up. 'What? You can't have. Don't be ridiculous.'

And suddenly, she felt really angry. 'I don't care what you or anyone else says, I *did* see him. I saw him in the park where we used to go. He was there, watching me.'

Again, John's face had settled into a mask. She couldn't read what he was thinking.

'And so,' he said slowly. 'Because of what you thought you saw … '

'What I *know* I saw.' Her voice was louder now.

'*Thought* you saw,' he repeated, 'you started meddling in matters that don't concern you.'

'How dare you say they don't concern me,' she said. 'He's my dad. I needed to know what had happened.'

John sighed. 'Kelly. You must stop this. You are only upsetting yourself.'

She ignored him. 'There were things that didn't make sense. Gaps … '

Kelly noticed that John's hands were gripping his knees really tightly.

'What are you talking about?'

Now I've started, I'll have to tell him everything and just hope I'm doing the right thing.

'Gran's diary, with all the pages cut out.'

'You read your gran's diary?!'

She didn't even register the shock in his voice. She was on a roll.

'And the fight at the pub just before he left … and his background. Jobs he'd had at random places, jobs he was over-qualified for. And his last painting.'

'His last painting?'

But she continued. 'And then the man following Jack.'

Uncle John suddenly betrayed some emotion in his face.

'Where is Jack?' asked Kelly again.

John hesitated. 'We'll make sure Jack is safe.'

There was a long silence as they stared at each other. Then John rose and put another log on the fire.

When he'd finished, he remained standing, his back to the fire and his arms folded. Still he said nothing.

'Gran knows something, doesn't she?'

Kelly was watching him carefully, waiting for him to ridicule her. But still he was silent. Then, at last, he seemed to come to a decision.

'What you and Jack have been doing,' he said, 'is very dangerous. *Very* dangerous indeed. And I want you to promise me that you will stop it. Immediately.'

'Why should we stop? I want to find out what happened to my dad. What *really* happened. What had he done that was so bad he had to disappear?'

'What? What do you mean?'

'Jack thinks he'd done something bad and he got rumbled. That's why he had to disappear.'

John knelt down in front of Kelly and took her hands. 'Please, Kelly. I'm begging you to stop this. You are meddling in something you don't understand and you are upsetting yourself. I'm sorry, but your dad is dead.'

She let him keep hold of her hands and she replied quietly.

'If you want us to stop, then you've got to level with us. What do you know? What does Gran know? And,' she added, 'why it is dangerous for us to go on trying to find out?'

He gently withdrew his hands and stood up.

'Listen to me, Kelly. Dad is dead. You are *never* going to see him again. Forensics have identified his remains.'

'That could be a lie. To put people off the scent.'

John laughed. 'Now you're being ridiculous.'

'OK,' said Kelly slowly. 'Then if he's dead, nothing can

hurt him, can it? So why can it do any harm to try and find out about why he did what he did? What changed him? Until a few weeks before he died, he was happy.'

'How can you know that? You were only a child.'

'I've been looking at some old family videos. After that fight in the pub, after that date, he was behaving differently.'

'Well, maybe he was. He was depressed. Severely depressed.'

'He was unhappy because he knew he was going to leave us,' she said.

John frowned. 'What do you mean?'

'Something he said to me,' she said quietly. 'And the note he left me behind the last painting he did.'

John looked up sharply, then he started pacing up and down. While Kelly was watching him, she thought she heard a very faint noise coming from the garden. Just the faintest rustle outside the window, which could easily have been the wind in the bushes.

'There's someone else here, isn't there?' she asked. 'There must be. The fire was alight and the lamp was on when we arrived.'

John stopped pacing and looked at her. 'No. There's no one here now. The man who lives here lit the fire for me, but he's gone away now.'

'So you'd been planning it. Planning to get me here?'

He stopped suddenly and stood still. He seemed to have come to a decision.

'OK,' he said. 'Let me tell you something about your dad, so that you can begin to understand.'

Kelly swallowed. Her mouth was really dry and every

muscle ached from the biking, but she didn't dare ask for even a glass of water. She leant forward.

'Did he do something really bad?'

'No … but he was in a lot of trouble.'

Kelly drew in her breath. 'What sort of trouble?'

John hesitated for so long that she thought he'd forgotten her. Then, at last, he cleared his throat.

'What I'm going to tell you, Kelly. It must go no further. You must tell no one. Do you understand?'

'What? Is it something even Mum doesn't know?'

'Not even your mum.'

'And Gran?'

He hesitated. 'Your gran knows,' he said quietly.

'I knew it!' said Kelly. 'I knew she's been hiding stuff from me, the old witch.'

John cleared his throat. 'You'll understand more when I tell you about your dad.'

Kelly's hands balled into fists. Was he going to tell her the truth at last? She hardly dared to breathe.

'Your dad,' said John slowly, 'was an agent. He worked for a very secret anti-terrorist organisation. More secret than MI5. He was recruited when he was a student at university.'

Kelly's eyes widened. This was something she really really hadn't expected.

'What?! What organisation?'

'I can't tell you that, Kelly. Only a few people know of its existence.'

Kelly frowned. 'Did you know what he was doing?'

John shook his head. 'I didn't know for a long time. Our parents gave him a lot of grief about not using his electronics degree and about taking random jobs so he could paint. But he ignored them. And me? I thought he was an idiot, I'm afraid.'

'Was that why you fell out?'

John nodded. 'I thought he was wasting his life. I had no idea what important work he was doing.'

'What *was* he doing?'

'He didn't tell me much, Kelly, but I know he saved a lot of lives.'

Kelly frowned. 'But … how?'

'To be honest, I don't know exactly, I think he was put into places where it was suspected that there were terrorist cells. He planted listening devices, eavesdropped on conversations, got to hear things and passed on information. That sort of thing.'

Kelly shivered. 'It sounds well dangerous.'

John nodded. 'He was very brave. I only wish I'd … '

'Was he still doing that sort of stuff when he disappeared.'

John shook his head. 'No. He'd pretty well stopped. The painting was going well and he didn't want to put the family at risk.'

'So … not stopped completely?'

John shook his head slowly. 'There was one last job. One that only he could do. He was the only one who had the contacts. It was big, that's all I know. He didn't tell me about it, but I knew it would save hundreds, probably thousands, of lives. And I knew something had gone wrong.'

Suddenly Kelly looked up. 'How come you know all this, Uncle John?'

John sat down again. 'Yes, I thought you'd ask that.'

'Well?'

John sighed. 'Your dad came to see me just before he disappeared. It was against the rules; he wasn't supposed to tell anyone what was happening, but he wanted someone in the family to know the truth before he went. Someone he trusted.' He put his hand through his hair. 'You know, for all our differences, we were brothers. He knew I'd tell no one.'

'Why didn't he tell Mum?'

John shook his head. 'He couldn't bear to.'

Kelly felt the tears welling up. 'Poor Mum,' she whispered.

'He knew that he was going for good, that he'd never be back. He wanted her to have a new life.'

'And Nat and me.'

'Yes, and you, too.'

'So, said Kelly. The job that went wrong … '

'Somehow he came under suspicion. We don't know how. But there were some very dangerous people he was dealing with. When they found out … '

'He had to go. To make sure they didn't get at us?'

'Exactly. If he was still alive, those people would have had no scruples. They would have used his family to try and get at him.'

Kelly shifted in her seat. 'So, are you saying he took his own life to save us?'

There was a slight hesitation while John cleared his throat. 'Yes,' he said.

Why don't I believe you?

'So, why has someone been following Jack?'

'There are still dangerous people out there who were very

angry about what your dad did. Jack's dad works for a national newspaper and we think these people have made the connection from Jack's dad to Jack and to you. They know Jack's been seeing you, been looking into your dad's past and maybe they think there's some big story brewing.' Uncle John looked away. 'Maybe they think your dad didn't really die – though, now that his remains have been found, I can't understand why.'

Kelly frowned.

This doesn't make sense.

'But how did you know we were looking into Dad's past?'

'I ... well, I ... '

He can't answer me! I don't trust him. Something's not right here.

'Where's Jack? I want to see him.'

'Trust me, he's safe.'

But I don't trust you.

They were silent, looking at one another. Again, Kelly thought she heard something moving outside and then an almost imperceptible creaking sound. She shivered, despite the warmth from the fire.

'Thank you,' she said quietly. 'Thank you for telling me all this Uncle John. It's ... well, it's a lot to take in.'

He nodded. 'I know.'

'Do you think I could I have a drink?'

'Um. Yes, sure. Tea be OK? I'll put the kettle on.'

John got up and walked slowly into the kitchen, which was at the far end of the cottage.

Kelly heard him filling the kettle.

She got up very quietly and walked rapidly into the passage, hesitated for a couple of seconds to check that John hadn't followed her, then headed for the back door. Very quietly, she withdrew the bolt at the top of the door, turned the handle and crept out into the garden.

The moon had risen and she could just make out an overgrown path leading down to some sort of shed at the bottom of the garden. Carefully, she closed the back door behind her and started off down the path, her eyes adjusting slightly to the darkness.

Quick, Kelly. John will realise you've gone. He'll come after you any minute.

There was complete silence now. Kelly could only hear the sound of her own breathing. If there was someone out here, they must have heard her footsteps and would be listening, waiting.

P'raps I'm imagining it. P'raps there's no one there. In which case, there's nothing to be scared of, is there?

But she *was* scared. She swallowed nervously as she felt her way forward, trying to avoid the sharp brambles. In places, she could see that they'd been flattened.

So someone has been here, walked down this path, crushing the brambles. Was it the man Uncle John told her about? The man who had lit the fire for him and turned on the lamp?

She fought her way through to the shed, conscious that she only had seconds before John came out. There was no time for hesitation, no more time to be quiet. She reached the door to the shed and her fingers fumbled over its surface until she found a latch. She didn't allow herself to think of the consequences as she yanked the door open and stood in the doorway.

Faintly, she could hear John calling her. She could just make out his words.

'You OK, Kelly?'

He must think she'd gone to the toilet again.

It was so dark that she couldn't make out what was inside. Then suddenly she remembered her phone. She pulled it out of her pocket and switched it on, relieved that the light still worked and was just about strong enough to reveal what was inside the shed.

There was something there. She was sure of it. Something or *someone*.

At first she couldn't make anything out, it was just a feeling, a sense of another being. Carefully, methodically, she played the light from her phone all around the inside of the shed.

It had been converted into a study, with a desk and a chair, and various bits of electronic kit.

There was no one there.

She heard the back door of the cottage open and the sound of Uncle John's voice.

'Kelly, you out there?' Then, louder. 'Where are you? What the hell are you doing?'

She was about to turn back, face Uncle John, when she heard something. What was it? She couldn't tell. A breath? A tiny movement?

Her lips were dry and her words sounded hoarse. 'Who's there?'

Her hand was shaking as she played the light all round the shed again, but this time she moved further inside so that she could focus the beam underneath the desk.

There *was* someone! Crouched under the desk, huddled against the wall.

She let out a cry and nearly dropped the phone.

She stumbled back out through the door, her heart pounding, and collided with Uncle John. He grabbed hold of her shoulders.

'Come away, Kelly,' he said. 'Come back into the house.'

But she twisted away from him.

There must be a light switch.

She felt up and down the wall by the door and at last she found it. The shed was suddenly flooded with light.

Uncle John tried to grab her but she lashed out at him, pushing him away from her with all her strength.

'Leave me alone!' she yelled.

John lost his balance and stumbled, giving Kelly just enough time to kneel down and peer under the desk.

'Who are you?' she shouted. 'What are you doing here?'

A man crawled out from under the desk. He stood up. He was very tall.

'Don't be scared. I won't hurt you,' he said.

Who is he?

The man put out a hand towards her, but she shrank back.

'Please don't be frightened.'

There was something familiar about the voice.

'Get away from me,' she hissed.

The man gasped and stepped back.

John had recovered his balance and was behind her.

'Come on Kelly,' he said. She could hear the fury in his voice.

But Kelly didn't move. 'Who is he?' she asked. 'What's he doing here?'

'No one you need to worry about, Kelly. Come on, let's get you into the warm.'

She glanced back as John started to steer her out of the door and, as she did so, she saw the man in the shed make this gesture, achingly familiar, putting both his hands up to his face and rubbing it, then letting his arms flop to his sides.

She stopped, refusing to be pushed further down the path, wriggled away from Uncle John and turned back, crashing through the door of the shed and slamming it behind her.

The man was still standing there, his hands loose at his side.

It was … but it wasn't.

'Dad?' she whispered.

John was pounding on the door, but Kelly put all her weight against it and turned the key in the lock. She stood staring at the man.

There was a long, long silence. Kelly didn't take her eyes off him.

He met her eyes and she could see that he was trying to control the emotion in his face.

His face! It wasn't her dad's face!

'Dad?' she said again.

Very slowly, he nodded. He put his hand up to his face. 'I've had a lot of surgery.'

Suddenly all the hurt, all the misery of those four years, boiled over in fury.

'How *dare* you!' she shouted at him. 'How dare you do this to us. How *could* you? How could you do this to Mum – and to me and Nat?

Uncle John was still banging on the door.

Kelly launched herself at the man in the shed, pounding him in the chest, yelling at him, tears pouring down her cheeks.

'Don't you realise,' she said, between sobs, 'Don't you know what you've done to us all? Have you any idea what we've been through?'

'Yes,' he said quietly. 'Yes, I know. And believe me, Kell, if there had been any other way ... '

'Don't call me Kell. That's what my family call me.'

She drew away then and saw the pain in the face that was – but wasn't – her dad's.

He was gazing at her, not trying to touch her, and she was standing in front of him, gulping back her sobs, no longer able to speak.

Uncle John's voice came through the door, muffled and furious.

'For god's sake, open the door!'

But neither Kelly nor her dad heard him.

Very slowly, Kelly inched forwards. Her dad held his arms out to her, tentatively, shyly, not in the way that he would have before, not the instinctive movement of a man who knew he was loved, expected affection, standing ready to give a big bear hug.

And it was his uncertainty that reached out to her. His knowing that he didn't deserve her affection, hadn't earned it. It was this that moved her and dissolved her anger, so that she finally let herself walk into his embrace.

She didn't know how long she stood there. She was sobbing uncontrollably now, held fast in his arms. He was crying, too.

'I'm so sorry,' he kept repeating. 'I'm so sorry.'

At last, her dad moved away and opened the shed door.

Kelly had never seen her uncle so angry as he faced his brother. 'What have you done? This is going to ruin everything.'

'She knew me,' Dad said quietly.

Suddenly there was the harsh sound of a mobile ringing.

John fished it out of his pocket. 'Yes?'

He listened for some time, nodding and sometimes saying a few words. Kelly's dad looked over Kelly's head at him.

When, at last, he snapped his phone shut, he let out a huge sigh.

'It's over,' he said. 'We've got him. And the others.'

Dad sat down and put his head in his hands. 'Thank God,' he said quietly.

'What's happening,' said Kelly, her voice beginning to rise. 'And where's Jack?'

'Jack will be fine. I promise you,' said John.

'You keep *saying* that! Where is he, what's happened to him?'

John looked across at his brother.

Dad reached out and took Kelly's hand, squeezing it tight. 'Tell her,' he said. 'There's no point in keeping it from her.'

There was a long silence, then John sighed.

'All right,' he said. 'I suppose we'll have to now. But not out here. Let's go back into the cottage.'

They walked back up the path and went inside. Kelly sat at her dad's feet, leaning against his knees, so many emotions whirling about in her head, but she forced herself to concentrate on what Uncle John was saying.

'The outfit that your dad was working for – the special anti-terrorist unit – well, somehow they found out that he had confided in me before he disappeared. Goodness knows how, but to cut a long story short, they recruited me, too.'

Kelly looked up. 'What?'

Uncle John nodded. 'I only do a bit of low-level stuff for them, nothing like what Dad did. Anyway, apart from me, only a handful of people knew what your dad was doing – and all of them were working on the inside – for the organisation.'

'Then … what happened? Why … ?'

Dad interrupted. 'It got out. Somehow, information was leaked.'

'Was it when you had that fight, in the pub?' asked Kelly. 'Is that when it happened?'

Dad nodded. 'A member of a terrorist cell found out what I was doing and that I was onto him and his associates. He was someone I'd befriended. He trusted me, and when he found out what I was doing, he came after me.'

Dad looked into the fire. 'When he walked into that pub I knew something was wrong. I knew he suspected me; his body language, the way his eyes shifted. I tried to act normal, the way I'd been trained, but I could see he had a gun and I had to think very quickly.'

'A gun!' said Kelly. 'So, was he going to kill you?'

'Oh yes,' said Dad quietly. 'I managed to get it from him, but then he started hitting me, and when people came to help me, he ran off. But then I knew it would only be a matter of time before he, or one of his associates, hunted me down.'

'So that's why you had to leave?'

Dad nodded. 'There was no choice,' he said quietly.

'They didn't know how much I knew about their activities. They had no idea. But they were going to stop me finding out more – and if they couldn't get me, they'd go after my family. So, I had to disappear, and not only disappear, but die.'

'And after that,' interrupted John, 'Only a very few people knew that he was still alive.'

Kelly swallowed. 'OK, I sort of get it. But what's happened now? What's changed?'

Dad looked across at John. 'What's changed,' he said slowly, 'is that the people who want to track me down have found out that I didn't die.'

There was a heavy silence.

'Is … is that because Jack and me started trying to find out … ?'

'No. No, not that. Though it probably didn't help.'

'Then what?'

'Despite all the checks we make, someone has slipped in under the net. Someone from a terrorist cell has infiltrated our organisation and has found out that I didn't die after all.'

'So, who's been following Jack?'

Uncle John looked up. 'Someone from the terrorist group has been following him. Though we've had you both under surveillance, too,' he added.

Kelly nodded. 'Jack recognised the guy from the pub when he saw him at the velodrome … '

Dad smiled. 'He's a good sleuth, that young man!'

Uncle John nodded. 'Seems so. But we needed to protect you both – and also flush out the informer – the mole, if you like. We still didn't know where the leak had come from, though we had our suspicions.'

'And now,' said Dad, 'our suspicions have been confirmed. There's been a huge round-up and the informer's details are on one of the terrorist's phones.'

'So, is it all over now, Dad?' asked Kelly. 'Can you come home?'

Dad put his hands on her shoulders. 'No, love,' he said quietly. 'I'll never be able to come home.'

Kelly twisted round to look at him. 'But why not! You're safe now, aren't you?'

She felt the tears coming again.

Uncle John watched them for a moment, father and daughter, looking at each other.

He turned away.

'We put out the story about Dad's ... remains being found. We thought it would stop any more investigation in its tracks, stop any bad guys thinking he might still be alive.'

'But it didn't, did it?'

John shook his head.

'Mum believed it,' said Kelly quietly.

'Oh God,' said Dad, looking at the floor. 'I'm so sorry.'

Kelly turned to Uncle John. 'Is this why you invited us up here for Christmas?'

John nodded. 'Yes, this has been planned for a while. We knew that if the bad guys still thought that dad was alive, after it had been announced that his remains had been found, this meant that there was definitely a mole in the organisation reporting back to them.'

'So, it was a sort of sting operation?'

Dad smiled. 'Sort of.'

Uncle John interrupted. 'Your dad wanted a chance to

get a glimpse of his family, make sure you were OK. That's why I asked you all up here.'

Kelly turned to Dad. 'You've been spying on us?'

Dad smiled. 'Let's just say that I've been keeping an eye on you.'

Kelly changed the subject. 'So what happened then, with Jack?'

'This terrorist cell,' said John. 'When Jack started asking questions at that pub, they made the connection between Jack and his dad. They thought that Jack's dad knew something, was on to a story about Dad not being dead. It's because he works for a big London newspaper now. And when Jack came up here – well, they reckoned if they took Jack, his dad would squeal and tell them all he knew.'

'Which is nothing,' said Kelly.

'Exactly. The poor guy was horrified when he was contacted.'

There was a long silence.

'So,' said Kelly slowly. 'You said we – me and Jack – had been under surveillance.'

'Yes. But you won't have seen anyone.'

'In the woods,' said Kelly, 'when I was walking the dog.'

John nodded. 'Someone was there.'

'And, on the beach this afternoon.'

He nodded again. 'And that was when we saw the guy bundle Jack into his car, and we followed him. But we couldn't pick him up until after we'd rounded up the rest of the gang. We couldn't risk him warning them.'

'What was he going to do to Jack?'

'Kidnap him. Keep him prisoner. Question him,' said John curtly.

In the silence that followed, Kelly tried not to think what that meant.

Dad broke the silence. 'I can't stay in the country any longer,' he said quietly. 'I have to leave now. Too much damage has been done.' He stroked Kelly's hair, then tucked a stray lock of it behind her ear. 'And this time I won't come back.'

Kelly turned to him. 'What?'

Dad reached over and squeezed her hand. 'Kell, I've been working under cover. I look different, don't I? Even you didn't recognise me. But now I'm going to leave the country. I've got another identity. We don't know who else knows I'm still alive. If there's the slightest chance I'm uncovered by terrorists, then you and Mum and Nat – and even Gran – might be in dreadful danger.'

She stared at him for a long time. 'It was you ... at the park, wasn't it?'

He nodded. 'I've come back a few times, to see that you are all doing OK. It was foolish of me, I know, but I just couldn't bear ... '

'And now?'

He looked away, biting his lip. 'And now,' he said softly, 'I have to disappear for ever. I was waiting until we knew for certain who the informer was. Until it was safe to make new plans.'

'Aren't you going to see Mum?'

Dad swallowed. 'I *can't*,' he whispered.

Uncle John intervened. 'She has to be allowed to get on with her life, Kelly, you must see that.'

'You mean I have to keep this secret all to myself?'

'I know it's a lot to ask,' said Dad. 'Do you think you can do it?'

'What? Say nothing to Mum or Nat?'

Both men were looking at her. The only sound in the room was from the fire, the wood crackling in the flames.

If I don't keep quiet, what then?

It began to dawn on her what could happen if she didn't. Mum would never be able to form a new relationship knowing Dad was still alive, Nat would be desperate to see his dad again – and there was always the risk he'd let something slip. There was so much at stake.

'It's one hell of an ask,' she said slowly. 'But I'll have to keep the secret, won't I?'

She sensed Dad's shoulders drop in relief.

Uncle John bent down and patted her arm. 'You can talk to me, Kelly. And Jack knows too much now. He's an exceptional young man and we'll have to trust him – and his dad. And there's always your gran.'

'Gran? All I really know is she's a good actor and that she cut pages out of her diary.'

'And why would she have done that, do you think?'

'I dunno, do I? Surely she's not … '

Dad smiled. 'There's a lot you don't know about your gran,' he said.

Twenty

There was so much pretending. To Mum, to Aunt Emma, to Nat. It was just as well that they were all bound up with other things. Mum was getting closer to Mark's dad all the time, and even though it broke her heart to admit it, Kelly could see how happy he made her. Aunt Emma was busy entertaining them and Nat was off on rides or talking about bikes with Ned.

But there was no way Jack couldn't know the truth. Jack had been kidnapped, hit and interrogated. He'd come face-to-face with one of the main terrorists.

When he'd been rescued and Uncle John and Kelly had picked him up from one of the other agents, he'd been too traumatised to speak, and it had been almost impossible to hide his state from Mum. He told her he'd had a bad fall off his bike – and the bruise where he'd been hit convinced her. Uncle John spent time debriefing him, making sure he understood how important it was to keep quiet about what had happened. And he was told everything. And so was his dad.

'It will take a long time for you to recover, Jack,' said Uncle John. 'And if you need to talk to anyone, please get in touch with me.'

Kelly never left his side for the remaining time they were in Suffolk, and she was sensible enough not to press him to tell her what had happened when he'd been kidnapped.

Then, just before they left, he seemed more like his old self.

'I can't believe you actually saw your dad,' he said to Kelly, when they were alone in the cottage.

'Yeah. It was really weird. You know, I didn't recognise him, not at first.'

'You sure it was him? They weren't playing some twisted trick on you?'

She shook her head. 'I'm sure,' she said quietly.

Jack reached out for her and she hesitated for a moment, then walked into his arms. He didn't try and kiss her, but just held her and stroked her hair.

'I wish I knew what to say,' he muttered.

Gently, Kelly prised herself away from him. 'You know, the greatest thing is knowing you know. Having someone on my side. Someone I can always talk to about it. And,' she added, 'knowing what you did for me.'

He smiled. He couldn't stop smiling.

'I might see Dad again,' said Kelly. 'Some day.'

'How? I thought he was going to Australia or somewhere.'

'He never said where he was going,' she replied.

'Of course he wouldn't, would he. So how? How would you keep in touch?'

Kelly shook her head. 'There are ways.'

'Yeah?'

She smiled. 'But that's something I really can't tell you about.'

'Fair enough. Does your gran know?'

'No. Not even Gran.'

Kelly kept going over all that had happened.

So much had been revealed when Uncle John and Dad had talked to her. Such as how Dad and Mum had really met. Not on a bus, as Mum had said. Well, it was, but Dad had engineered it. He knew Gran before he met Mum. Gran had worked for the same organisation, and it was *she* who had recruited him. She wasn't to know that he'd seen her one day with her daughter (Mum) and fallen in love. It had taken him no time to suss out her daily movements and it had been easy to jump off her regular bus one day and knock her bags out of her hand.

Of course, when Gran had found out that Mum and Dad were going out she was furious, but there was nothing she could say without revealing her own role to Mum.

And later, going for a long walk with John, Kelly heard about what her dad had been doing and how many terrorist operations had been stopped because of his undercover work.

'You never hear about all the atrocities that *didn't* happen,' said John. 'You only hear about it when a terrorist group succeeds and lives are lost.'

She supposed that was true. People like Dad and his

222

colleagues were sacrificing everything to keep people safe. How could she be anything but proud of him?

She'd told Jack everything they'd told her. Well, *almost* everything.

'What's going to happen to the terrorist group?'

'They've all been arrested.'

'And the informer?'

I asked John about him and he said that the organisation was pretty unforgiving to people like him, whatever that means. I guess he'll have to answer a lot of questions, too.'

'Like whether there's anyone else out there who knows your dad is still alive?'

She nodded. 'Trouble is, he probably won't let on. That's why Dad has to go away. Even though he looks so different, it's too risky for him to stay. He's got another new name and another new identity, but I don't know what it is. Even Uncle John doesn't know.'

'How do you feel about all this?'

Kelly took a while to answer. She sighed and looked away, out of the window at the darkening sky.

'Strange.'

'What do you mean?'

'You know I told you that when I first saw him, I didn't recognise him?'

Jack nodded.

'Well, although I know it *is* him, it's as if … oh I can't explain … as if the old dad *did* die. I don't feel quite the same about this new dad. All the stuff in his life he never told us about. Aren't your parents supposed to be honest with you? And never mind not telling me, he never told *Mum*!'

'Are you saying that you won't feel so bad about not seeing him again?'

Kelly frowned. 'It's as though I've stepped back from him. He can't come back into our lives now – and I'm not sure I'd want him to, this other dad, even if he could. I don't feel I really know him any more.'

Jack didn't say anything and Kelly continued. 'It's four years. *He's* changed. *We've* changed. I can't hang onto that memory of who he was. That Dad no longer exists. And Mum – she's got another chance to be happy. It's not fair to deny her that.'

'But I feel sort of empty, too. I know what's happened, I know I was right to sense he was still alive, but I … well, I sort of want to let him go now. If he can't be the old dad, can't be part of the family, what's the point in hanging onto this memory of him?

'Are you glad you saw him?'

'Yeah. Really, really glad.'

'It's laid the ghost?'

She nodded. 'That's exactly right. It's laid the ghost.'

'Will he know what's happening to you – and your mum and gran and Nat?'

'Yes. He explained it to me. He's always known. He told me that the organisation is really good at that. They've kept him informed. And they'll keep on keeping him informed – about anything important that happens to us.'

'What about your gran?'

'What about her?'

'How much does she know?'

Kelly laughed. 'Everything, I guess. Dad said she would have suspected, from the start, what had happened. That's why she was so angry. She knew there was always a chance Dad would get found out and have to disappear, and then she'd have to pick up the pieces.'

'Will you talk to her about it?'

'Nah. She knows *I* know. I know *she* knows. And we'll keep quiet about it. It's the only way.'

'But you'll talk to me about it?'

She took his hand and squeezed it. 'Yes. And that's so great, knowing you know. That I don't have to pretend with you.'

They stood there for a while, looking at each other and smiling, then Kelly looked away.

'Jack?'

'Yeah.'

'Whatever happens to us, will you promise me you will never, *ever*, say anything about all this to anyone else?'

'You know I won't.'

Then he pulled her towards him again.

It was their last day in Suffolk and they were at Uncle John's house. Just before they left, Jack looked carefully at Kelly's painting, which was now hanging up above the fireplace. He stared at it, screwing up his eyes, and then he smiled.

You'd only see the words if you looked really hard. The picture was of the park near Kelly's home, full of vibrant colours and very impressionistic, and the words were disguised among swirling leaves and branches, so that they were almost indistinguishable – unless you were looking for them.

Jack found them and gasped at how cleverly they'd been integrated into the picture.

He is not dead.

Six months later

Kelly and Lizzie were walking to school.

'Hey, you look happy! What's with that great grin all over your face?'

Kelly laughed. 'Nothing. It's a lovely day and the weekend's coming.'

'Don't give me that, Kelly Wilson. Something's happened.'

There is something, Lizzie, but I can't tell you.

'It's Jack. You've fallen in love with him – finally.'

Kelly was still smiling. 'Umm. Maybe just a bit.'

'I knew it!'

Kelly tried to wipe the smile off her face. It wasn't fair to Lizzie. Lizzie and Mark hadn't been getting on that well and finally Mark had broken it off. Lizzie said she wasn't bothered, but Kelly knew her too well, could sense the hurt beneath the brave face. Lizzie had told her how Mark had pushed her to take their relationship further, even though Lizzie had told him she wasn't ready. Then there was the attention he attracted from other girls, attention he lapped up eagerly.

It was awkward. Mark's dad and Kelly's mum were an item and Mark was often at their house, so Kelly saw a lot of Mark and of his sister, and although she got on fine with them, she resented how Mark had treated her best friend.

I'm glad he never fancied me. He's too good-looking. It's all too easy for him.

But today, nothing could spoil her day, even though she couldn't tell anyone why she was so happy.

This was the day when she knew she'd hear from Dad.

As soon as she got home she picked up the free copy of the local newspaper which had come through the door. No one usually read it, so no one noticed when she took it up to her bedroom.

She opened it at the personal ads page, and there it was. A message that only she and Dad would understand, something they'd worked out before he left.

Every six months, on the tenth of the month. That was what they'd agreed. Not on birthdays, not on any significant day, just the tenth day of the month, in June and December.

It didn't take her long to find it.

'Arise fair sun and kill the envious moon.'

She recognised it immediately.

Kelly smiled. She'd half expected him to put 'parting is such sweet sorrow', but maybe that would have been too obvious.

She sighed and put the paper down on her lap, smoothing over the words with her finger.

As long as the quote was from Romeo and Juliet, everything was all right.

It meant he was well – and safe.

Rosemary Hayes lives in Cambridgeshire with her husband and an assortment of animals. She worked for Cambridge University Press and then for some years ran her own publishing company, Anglia Young Books. She has written over forty books for children, in a variety of genres and for a variety of age groups. Her first novel, 'Race Against Time' was runner up for the Kathleen Fidler Award and since then many of her books have won or been shortlisted for awards.

Rosemary also runs creative writing courses at an Adult Education Centre.

Visit her website: www.rosemaryhayes.co.uk
Follow her on twitter: @HayesRosemary
Read her blog: www.rosemaryhayes.co.uk/wpf